Pilgrim's Progress
An Adventure Book

Chris Wright

WHITE
TREE
PUBLISHING

Pilgrim's Progress
An Adventure Book

Chris Wright

ISBN 13: 978-0-9525956-6-3

First Published in the United State of American 2007
by Lighthouse Christian Publishing as
Pilgrim's Progress Puzzle Book © 2007 Chris Wright

This revised edition © 2012 Chris Wright

PUBLISHED BY
WHITE TREE PUBLISHING
28 FALLODON WAY
BRISTOL BS9 4HX
UNITED KINGDOM

For David, Eva, and Alexander

Books by Chris Wright for young readers
See back pages for more details

Agathos, The Rocky Island, and Other Stories
Mary Jones and Her Bible – An Adventure Book
Pilgrim's Progress – An Adventure Book
Pilgrim's Progress – Special Edition
Zephan and the Vision

INTRODUCTION

A pilgrim is someone who sets out on a special journey, and this is a story about some young pilgrims. John Bunyan wrote a book called *The Pilgrim's Progress* over three hundred years ago. This is his story, retold for young readers, with children taking the part of some of the main characters.

All through this book there are puzzles to solve and questions to answer. Some may be hard, and some will be easy. You don't have to solve each one before turning the page, but it will make the story more fun if you spend a little time trying to work out the answers. If you're stuck, the answer will be somewhere on the next page, often in bold type.

You may want to read this book again later, or lend it to a friend. So I suggest you don't write the answers on the pages, but use a piece of paper instead.

Chris Wright
Bristol
England

PART 1

CHRISTIAN'S JOURNEY

MY NAME IS CHRISTIAN. I used to live with my father in a terrible city called Destruction. There were just the two of us, because my mother was living with the King in the Celestial City. Of course, she wanted me and my father to join her there, but my father always said he was too busy with his work. So one day I decided to go there on my own.

My friends laughed, and said, "There is no King, and there's no Celestial City!" The only person who didn't laugh was my friend Christiana. She had to look after her four younger brothers, because both her parents were already living with the King.

I had a special Book. It told me that there really is a King, and he lives with his Son in the Celestial City. One day I met a man called Evangelist who explained how to get there. "Can you see a light shining a long way off?" Evangelist asked, pointing across the fields.

I said I thought I could see something.

"Go over the fields to the light," Evangelist said, "and when you get there you'll find a high wall, and a door in it with a Wicket Gate. Knock, and you'll be let in. But make sure no one tries to stop you on the way."

On the day I was leaving, some of my friends called and wanted me to play with them. I shook my head and told them I was going to see the King. I had a heavy weight on my back, but no one else could see it. I called it my burden, and my Book said the King's Son could remove it for me.

"You'll get lost," they said. "The path is very dangerous. There are lions and giants, and even dragons. Stay here with us."

But I'd made up my mind. "I'm going to the King," I told them, "and you can come with me if you like."

Two of my friends said they might as well give it a go. Their names were Obstinate and Pliable. Obstinate got his name because he always wanted to have his own way.

"Are you sure you know where you're going?" Obstinate asked me.

"I'm going to..." I stopped. I couldn't remember where I was going.

Across the fields,
Day or night,
Christian is going
To the shining _ _ _ _ _

What is the missing word?

Then it came back to me. **"I'm going to the shining light."**

The three of us had only walked a short way, when Obstinate said he was going back. Pliable, who usually did what Obstinate told him to do, said he would stay with me.

Obstinate looked ever so surprised, and he ran away in a bad temper.

As Obstinate disappeared from sight, my feet started sinking into some soft ground. I tried to pull myself free, but I kept sinking deeper and deeper into the horrible mud.

Pliable was already up to his knees, and he shouted in panic, "I'm sinking! I'm sinking! This marsh is sucking me under!"

That's when I remembered this place was called the Slough of Despond, where people often give up because they think it's hopeless to go any further. Somehow Pliable managed to pull himself out of the deep mud and ran home, leaving me stuck firmly in the Slough of Despond.

"Help me," I called, "Anybody, please help me!"

"Grab hold of my hand," I heard someone shout.

I looked round, and saw a boy reaching out to me. "My name is Help," the boy said. "Be quick and hold on tightly, before you sink any deeper."

Help pulled and pulled, and I slowly came free.

"What are you doing here?" Help asked, as soon as I was safe.

"I'm going to the shining light above the Wicket

Gate," I said. "But ... but I can't see it any more."

Help pointed across the fields. "There it is," he said. "Can you see it now?"

Yes, there it was, shining more brightly than the sun. "Is the way safe?" I asked. "This mud is bad enough, and my friends told me there are lions and giants and dragons along the way."

"Are you going to see the King?" Help asked.

"I am."

He smiled. "Then you need not be afraid. I have already been as far as the Gates to the King's City. Yes, you will meet all sorts of dangers on the way, but the King's Son will watch over you every step you take. He sent me here to rescue you from the Slough of Despond."

This made me feel happier, so I said goodbye to Help and walked towards the light. As I got closer, I heard another boy calling to me.

"Where are you going?" the boy asked.

"I'm going to see the King," I said. "Can you see a heavy load on my back? I want to get rid of it as soon as possible."

What can the boy can see on Christian's back?

The boy told me he could see **nothing**. "You don't want to go the King," he said, taking hold of my arm and sounding friendly. "It's very dangerous."

"Help promised the King's Son will watch over me," I said, and I hoped Help was telling the truth. I wasn't looking forward to meeting lions and giants and dragons on my own.

"My name is Worldly," the boy said. "Don't believe everything people tell you about the King. Can you see that high mountain?"

I looked to where young Worldly was pointing. "Yes."

"It's called Law Mountain. To climb it you have to always be doing good things and *never* making mistakes. If you manage to climb to the top, you'll see a town on the other side. I have some friends who live there. They'll soon help you forget all about the King and his City, and then you won't feel that burden on your back."

"I don't want to forget about the King," I said. "But perhaps you're right. Maybe I should try to climb the mountain."

Young Worldly smiled. "It's good for everyone to try. It will make you very happy."

"Will I see the light from the top?" I wanted to know. "I have to go to the light."

"Go to the top and find out," Worldly said with a smile.

Well, it sounded as though young Worldly knew what he was talking about, especially as he lived near Law Mountain.

The way up looked ever so steep, but there was a

clear path, so I imagined lots of people had been up it already. I wondered if any of them got to the top without going wrong. I had a feeling deep inside that no one had ever managed it.

Christian is climbing to the top,
And hopes to find the Way;
Is young Worldly helping him,
Or leading him astray?

So I started to climb, wishing my friend Christiana had come with me – but she was too busy looking after her four brothers. I hoped she'd come later, and we could meet in the King's City.

The path up the mountain got steeper and steeper, and a sudden thunder storm shook the rocks. For a moment I thought the rocks were going to fall on me, and I cried out in fright.

"Keep going," young Worldly called from the bottom of the path. "It may be hard now, but the King will be pleased to see you trying so hard."

I stopped in fright. "I don't want to go on," I said to myself, "but Help told me the way is difficult. Maybe this is what he meant, and I *have* to keep going. What shall I do?"

"Where are you going, Christian?" a man called out.

I held tightly to the rocks and turned round. Evangelist was standing in the path. "Young Worldly told me this is the way to the King," I said.

Evangelist shook his head. "Don't you remember that I told you to go to the light?"

My voice and my legs were shaking. "Worldly told me that this is the way," I said.

Evangelist shook his head. **"Worldly is leading you astray.** I warned you not to listen to anyone." Evangelist came close to me. "Go back down, Christian, and walk to the light above the little Wicket Gate."

So I turned round and walked back down the hill. And there, across the fields, I could see the light again, burning brightly even in the daylight.

I ran towards it, and as I got close I could see a notice, above a large door in the wall.

Christian's eyes are dazzled by the bright light which is making the sign look a strange shape. He has trouble reading the letters C, D and O. What does the notice say?

The notice says: *Knock, and the door will be opened to you.*

Who are these two boys, and where they are?

The picture shows Help pulling Christian out of the Slough of Despond.

"This must be the right place," I said aloud. "Evangelist told me to knock." So I knocked loudly.

"What do you want?" a man asked as he opened a small door inside the large one. It was called the Wicket Gate. The man had the kindest face I'd ever seen.

"My name is Christian, and I want to go to the King," I said "My mother is already with him."

"Then you must come in quickly." The man reached out and pulled me through the little Wicket Gate.

"Why did you do that?" I asked in surprise.

The man pointed to an arrow sticking in the ground, just outside the door. "My enemy shot that arrow at you," he said. "He gets angry when people want to come through here."

"Who are you?" I asked.

"They call me Goodwill," the man said. "The King is my Father, and this Wicket Gate is my door."

I felt very safe when I heard those words. "How do I get to your Father's City?" I asked.

Goodwill smiled "Stay here tonight, Christian, and tomorrow I will show you the Way to the Celestial City where my Father lives."

Christian has entered through the door,
And now is on the Way;
Should he keep on with his walk,
Or is it safe to stay?

I felt tired, and decided to stay for the night. Goodwill is the King's Son, so I knew I'd be safe. After a long night's sleep, I decided I was ready for any lion or giant I might meet. Maybe even ready for a dragon.

After breakfast, Goodwill took me outside and pointed along the road. "Keep close to the wall," he said, "and don't take any paths to the side. The Way to the King is always straight ahead. If you need to rest, you can stop at the large house you will come to in the middle of the day."

The morning air felt fresh, and I enjoyed the walk. So far there were no lions, no giants and no dragons. Everything seemed good.

The sun rose higher and higher in the blue sky, and I began to feel tired and hungry as the morning went on. I'd been walking for three hours.

"I wonder where the large house is," I said to myself. "I must be close."

And I was right. Not far ahead, between some trees, I saw the house. I went up to the front door and knocked.

The man who opened it told me his name was Interpreter, and he invited me in. "I can see you're one of the King's pilgrims," he said. "I have some food for you, but first there are some things that the King wants you to see."

He took me into a room and showed me a painting of someone he called the Good Shepherd, walking over a mountain path. All around the Good Shepherd, among the rocks, were thorns that had torn his clothing. In his arms the Shepherd carried a sheep.

"Was it lost?" I asked.

"Yes," Interpreter said. "Can you see how tired it looks, and how its fleece is torn? But the Good Shepherd heard its cry, and he never rested until he found it. And now he's carrying it home in his arms."

"It must have been a hard path," I said. "Look, the stones have cut the Shepherd's feet."

"It was a hard path, but he didn't mind, because he loved that sheep."

"Who is the Good Shepherd?" I asked. "He looks exactly like Goodwill."

Interpreter held the lamp high so I could see the picture more clearly. "The Good Shepherd is our King's Son, and he is the man who let you in at the Wicket Gate. Just as a shepherd loves his flock, so the King's Son loves you, Christian. The pilgrims are like that sheep. You must always remember who is watching over you."

"*I'm* a pilgrim now," I said, looking up at Interpreter. "And I was lost, just like that sheep."

"A pilgrim, and a sheep in the flock of the Good Shepherd," Interpreter said. "Tell me, Christian, **can you remember why the Good Shepherd went looking for the lost sheep?**"

"Because it was lost, and he loved it," I said, and Interpreter told me it was the right answer.

Interpreter's house had rooms with many exciting things to see. He showed me a room where a man was sweeping a dusty floor. But as the man used the brush, the dust rose in the air and made us sneeze.

A servant hurried in with some water and splashed it all over the floor. Then the dust settled and the man was able to sweep the room clean.

"The room is like us," Interpreter explained. "There is no way we can make ourselves good enough to please the King. The more we try to do it, the more we make a mess. The King's Son is the only one who can make our hearts clean."

We ate a good meal together, and soon I was back on the path, heading for the King's City. My burden had bothered me since I first read about the King and his Son in my Book. I thought I'd lose it as soon as I went through the Wicket Gate, but I knew it was still there.

Does it contain:

Some food and *drink* for his lunch?

All the things he has ever done *wrong* that have hurt the King?

All the things that worry him?

All the things *he* is afraid of?

Some spare clothes?

All the wrong things I had ever done were wrapped up in that bundle on my back, as well as my worries and the things I was afraid of. The weight was slowing me down, and I had to get rid of it as soon as possible.

As the day got hotter, the weight of the burden felt heavier and heavier. Presently I came to a small hill by the side of the road, with a Cross on the top. I began to climb the path to look at it, and just for a moment I imagined I could see someone hanging on it, his hands and feet bleeding.

As I looked, I felt the burden fall from my shoulders and heard it tumble to the bottom of the hill. I turned round and watched it fall into a deep pit and roll out of sight.

I was so surprised I could hardly believe that the person who had been on the Cross had made me lose the burden, for it had been such a trouble to me.

I stood wondering who was on the Cross.

Who did Christian see on the Cross? His name is hidden here:

THEre he stood in thanKs, knowING that hiS burden waS gONe for ever.

Check all the capital letters!

THE WICKET GATE

SLOUGH OF DESPOND

LAW MOUNTAIN

THE CITY OF DESTRUCTION

Can you find your way safely from the City of Destruction to the Wicket Gate, without going anywhere near Law Mountain or passing through the Slough of Despond?

"It was the King's Son" I said aloud. "Has my burden really gone?"

I waited a few minutes and there was no sign of it coming back. The King's Son had taken the weight from my shoulders for ever. It was such a wonderful feeling to know I would never see it again.

"Now I can walk as quickly as I like," I said to myself. But although the Cross was empty, I stayed by it for a long time, full of joy and thanks.

I remembered reading in my Book how the King's Son once came to live in the City of Destruction. Although he was loving and good, some of the people hated him. At last they put him to death by nailing him to a wooden cross. But he came alive again, and now lives in the Celestial City.

I stood quietly, knowing that this must be that Cross. It was here that the King's Son was punished, instead of me. The King would no longer be angry with me. As I looked, tears came into my eyes.

The top picture shows Christian at the Cross, just before he lost his burden. There are three changes in the second picture. Can you find them?

Christian has lost his burden, the grass has gone underneath the Cross, and the top of the Cross is shorter.

I heard voices behind me, saying, "We bring you peace."

I turned round quickly and saw three figures in robes that shone so brightly that the light hurt my eyes, and I had to look away.

"Christian, you have often displeased the King," the first one said, "but I have come to tell you that you are forgiven, and the wrong things you have done will not be remembered anymore."

I turned back to look again, for surely the only person who could forgive me like this was the King's Son. But the light still dazzled me.

The second figure said, "Christian, your clothes are torn and dirty. I wish my pilgrims to wear clothes that are clean, so I am giving you new ones."

And before I had time to think what to say, my old clothes were taken away and I found myself dressed in clothes from the King.

Then the third figure set the mark of the King on my forehead, and gave me a roll of parchment with a seal on it. He called it a Roll of Faith, with the Seal of Promise, and told me to read it and be sure to take care of it, for I would have to show it at the Gates of the Celestial City.

After this, the three went away, leaving me to rub my eyes and think about everything the King had done for me. I gave three leaps for joy and started to sing a song about the King's Son. I had lost my burden, and I belonged to the King forever – I really was one of the King's own children!

As I continued my journey in my new clothes, I came to a wall by the side of the Way. Two boys climbed over it, dropping onto the Way of the King and making me jump.

"Where have you two come from?" I asked in surprise.

The boys told me they were starting their journey to the Celestial City to see the King.

"But don't you know you have to come in at the Wicket Gate," I said, remembering what Evangelist has told me.

"Oh," the boys said, "everyone we know cuts across the fields and climbs over the wall. It's much easier."

The two boys are in the same place as Christian. So do you think it matters how you get onto the path?

The more I thought about it, the more sure I was that the King didn't want people starting their pilgrimage like this, so I said, "You're wrong. People can't do that."

That made them laugh. "Oh, don't you bother about it," they said. "Our people have been doing it for years. Anyway, does it matter, as long as we're on the right road now? You came through the Wicket Gate, and we came over the wall. We're all in the same place, aren't we?"

"I still don't think you should have done it," I said.

"That's nonsense," they told me. "We're just as good pilgrims as you are, except that you have such fine clothes, which we expect somebody had to give you, because your own were like rags!"

Those words hurt me, and I wanted to be rude back to them. But I'd read in my Book that the King's servants must speak gently, even when angry words are spoken to them.

So I waited a moment, then said quietly, "That's quite true. The King gave me these clothes because my own were indeed like rags. I'm glad he did, because now when I get to the King's City he'll know I'm one of his pilgrims. And I have this Roll of Faith to show at the end of my journey. Do you have one?"

The boys kept laughing and shook their heads. They smiled to each other as they walked with me to the foot of a steep hill. A signpost said this was Hill Difficulty, and its finger pointed to a narrow track that ran straight up. *The Way of the King*, it said. I could see two others paths running round each side of the hill. One path was marked *Danger* and the other had a sign saying *Destruction*.

The Way of the King was rocky and steep, but I had to take it. I looked back to see if the two boys were following me, but they'd already taken the other paths, one going to the right and the other to the left.

"What's the good of climbing up there?" they called out. "Our two paths are smooth and easy. They go round the hill. We'll see you on the other side."

Danger and *Destruction*. How could anyone read the names of those two paths, and still go along them? Surely the only safe path was the one going straight up the hill. Well, the two boys would have known – if they'd only taken the trouble to obey the King and begin their journey in the right way.

They could put on a show of following the Way of the King when things were easy, and now they thought they had found an easy path round the hill.

Christian's choice seems very hard,
When he starts up the hill;
Surely the paths will join up,
Do you think t _ _ y w _ _ l ?

Do you think they will? Well, I didn't think so. As I climbed Hill Difficulty, I look down to see what was happening to the two boys. One boy was following his path into a dark forest. Surely he would never find his way out.

The path on the other side of the hill, the one the other boy had chosen, led between two dangerous cliffs. The boy slipped and fell, cutting himself on some sharp rocks.

As I got near the top of the hill, two other boys came racing down towards me. "There are two huge lions on the path!" they shouted. "Quick, turn back before they eat you!"

I knew that the way to the King's City led up the hill, so I kept climbing. The higher I climbed, the darker the evening got, and the path was soon difficult to see.

Just before night came, I noticed a large house in the distance. I hurried towards it, hoping I could stay there for the night.

The path became more and more narrow, and suddenly I saw the two lions standing each side of the path. I stopped, wondering what to do, for there was only a small space between them. If I tried to slip through, I was sure they'd attack me.

"Don't be frightened," a man called out. "The lions are chained. Keep in the middle of the path, and they cannot hurt you."

The man had come from the house, so he probably knew what he was talking about. So I went on, even though I was afraid, taking care to keep in the very middle of the path. Then I noticed some chains holding the great creatures back. So although they roared as I walked between them, they were not able to stretch out their huge paws to touch me.

I passed the lions and ran to man. "This is one of the King's houses," the man said. "If you are a pilgrim you are very welcome, and can stay here tonight. Four young sisters live here. The whole family are friends of pilgrims."

I went into the house to meet the four sisters. "You must stay with us for a few days," they insisted. "Do you have your family with you?"

I shook my head. "My mother is already with the King in his City, and my father is too busy at work to travel."

"Do you have any friends with you?" they asked.

I shook my head again. "All my friends laughed at me when I told them I was going to find the King. No, not all my friends. Christiana didn't laugh, but she has four young brothers to look after. I'm hoping she will start her journey soon."

As I went up to my room, I stopped on the stairs. "What is the name of this house?" I asked.

The name of the house is:

lutituɒəᗺ əƨuoH ɘʜT

Can you read it backwards? You may need a mirror, or you can try looking through the page from the other side.

I spent three whole days at the **House Beautiful** learning about the King and his Son, for there was so much I didn't know. On the second day the sisters took me to a room filled with shining helmets, shields, armour of the finest metal, swords, and shoes that would never wear out.

"These are for pilgrims to use," the sisters told me.

I wanted a sword and shield of my own, so I could be one of the King's soldiers, but I kept quiet.

They then took me to a room full of books, where the sisters told the story of a boy called David, who fought with a great giant.

"The giant was called Goliath, and he was one of the King's enemies," they explained. "Goliath was covered with his own armour from head to foot. David wore only a shepherd's clothes, so the giant thought it would be easy to kill him."

"Didn't David have a sword and a spear?" I asked.

The sisters shook their heads.

"What did he fight with?" I wondered why anyone would try to fight a giant without any sort of weapon.

The sisters knew the answer. "David had a sling and a stone. When he threw the stone at the giant, the King helped him. The stone hit Goliath on the head and killed him. Then David cut the giant's head off with the giant's own sword."

That made me feel good. If the King helped David, he would surely be ready to help any other pilgrim who trusted in him.

When I woke up the next morning I looked out of my window. In the far distance I could see green hills and sparkling rivers, and the Way of the King ran right through the hills. Perhaps all my troubles were over, and there were no more dangers to face.

But I had a surprise after breakfast. "We have something for you," the sisters said, looking at each other and smiling. "Between this house and the King's City, the King's enemies can be very dangerous, so all the King's pilgrims need to be ready to fight."

They took me to the room full of armour. "These are for you," the sisters said, picking up some pieces that were the right size for me.

Christian is given six things. Which one on this list isn't he given?

SHIELD
SWORD
BREASTPLATE
KEY
CHARIOT
HELMET
SHOES

Christian is given everything, except the chariot.

"You must have this key, as well as the armour," one of
the sisters told me. "We call it the Key of Promise. There
are many promises hidden on it. One day you may need it
to escape from the darkness of a giant's dungeon."

I examined the key closely. I could see one promise:
'*I have come as Light into the world, so that everyone
who believes in Me will not remain in darkness.*'

As I went to the gates of the House Beautiful, the
man who helped me get past the lions called out, "There
is another young pilgrim not far ahead, although he
didn't stay here last night. His name is Faithful. If you
hurry, you will be able to catch him up."

I knew it would be good to travel with a friend, so I
hurried down the path.

"Wait for us," the four sisters called. "We'll go down
with you. The path is ever so slippery."

In spite of the warning I fell over four times, but I
didn't hurt myself badly. At the bottom of the hill the
sisters said they had to leave me, and I felt so alone – as
well as bruised. The valley was quiet and cool, and I
walked on quickly hoping to see Faithful in the distance.
But instead of finding Faithful, I came to a dark place
where I met a terrible monster with wings like a dragon.
Smoke and fire poured out of his body.

I was going to turn round and run back to the four
sisters, but I had a breastplate and shield to protect my
front – and nothing to protect my back. Perhaps the
creature would go past without noticing me.

I walked on steadily, and in a minute the thing was close.

"My name is the Destroyer," the monster roared, blocking the path and looking down at me. "I would like to know where you're going."

"To the City of the King," I said boldly.

The Destroyer smiled, but it wasn't a nice smile. "Don't be so foolish," he said. "I can be kind to people when I like them. You can live in my house and be one of my servants."

I shook my head "I'm one of the *King's* servants, so how can I go back with you?"

"Oh, that doesn't matter," the Destroyer said, still smiling. "I won't be angry with you."

I could feel my knees shaking, but I managed to say, "I love the King, and I'd rather be *his* servant than yours. Now, let me go on my way."

The King's enemy seemed to have made up his mind that I was going home with him. "Don't be silly," he said. "You've not been a good pilgrim since starting out. You've done things that have upset the King."

"I've told the King I'm sorry," I said, "and he's promised to forgive me."

Christian has some armor
To protect him from attack.
But if he turns and runs away,
What about his back?

The Destroyer became fierce with rage. "I hate your King, and I hate his Son," he screamed. "And I hate everybody and everything belonging to him. You're *my* servant now, Christian, and you will *never* get to the Celestial City – *because I'm going to kill you!*"

I decided it was safer to stay and fight, for **how could I protect my back if I ran away?** I only just had time to hold up my shield, before the Destroyer began to throw fiery darts. There were so many that they hit my shield like hail. That was when I remembered the story I heard at the House Beautiful, of David and the giant.

"David only had his shepherd's clothes," I said aloud, "and I have the sword and shield. I will trust in the King's Son, and not to be afraid. I belong to the King now."

So I held my shield firmly on my arm, and stopped nearly all the Destroyer's darts, although some hit my hands and feet. The evil enemy rushed at me and seized me in his strong claws, cutting into my arms and legs.

Then he flung me to the ground, and my sword fell from my hand. Just as the Destroyer tried to strike his last blow, I called to the King. At that moment I remembered some words in my Book spoken by the King's Son. *"Take courage, I have overcome the world."*

I realized that the sword was within my reach. I put out my hand and picked it up, and before the Destroyer had time to see what I was doing, I pushed it deep into his body.

The King's enemy can't bear the pain of a wound

given with one of the King's swords, and he screamed loudly. My courage returned, and I thrust the weapon at the enemy again. With a terrible roaring the Destroyer fled across the valley, leaving me alone.

I lay for a minute on the path, then stood up slowly and looked around. All over the grass I could see the sharp darts the Destroyer had thrown, but the King's enemy had gone.

"It was the King who helped me," I realized, my heart full of thanks.

But I'd been badly wounded. I fell onto the grass and rested my head against a great rock. After a few minutes I fell asleep, and dreamt that the King's Son was with me, rubbing my wounds with healing leaves.

When I woke up, I was amazed to see that my arms and legs had stopped bleeding and didn't even hurt.

I knew I have to hurry away from there, for perhaps the Destroyer would come back to look for me again.

Keeping my sword in my hand, and looking carefully from side to side among the rocks and bushes, I continued along the Way of the King.

Can you remember what two things poured out of the Destroyer's body, when he met Christian?

(Look back for the answer.)

I was glad I stayed to fight the Destroyer. I had no armour for my back, and those fiery darts would have hit me, instead of landing on my shield.

Soon I came to a small hill, and climbed up to see what was ahead. Not far away I could see a boy about my age, so I ran as fast as I could and quickly caught up with him. But in my rush I raced past, unable to stop. The next thing I knew I was flat on the ground!

The boy laughed as he helped me to my feet. He said his name was Faithful, and he was going to the King's City. I remembered seeing him in the City of Destruction, and I told him I would be a good idea if we travelled together now.

"I wanted to leave the City of Destruction when you did, Christian," Faithful said, as we walked along, "but you left in such a hurry that I couldn't catch up with you. So I've been walking by myself."

"Did you stay long?"

"Only a few days. Everybody was talking about you, and I kept wishing I'd left when you did."

"What were people saying about me?" I wanted to find out, for I was surprised that anybody had even noticed I'd gone.

Faithful looked embarrassed. "Well," he said, "if you must know, most of them said you were stupid."

I laughed. "I don't mind. That's what they kept telling me when I lived there. What happened to Pliable, after he got stuck in the marsh with me?"

"When his friends heard he'd only gone that far, they made fun of him for turning back."

"That's strange," I said, frowning. "They laughed at me because:

and they laughed at Pliable because:

You must read each word backwards.

Yes, they laughed at me because **I kept going**, and they laughed at Pliable because **he went back**!

* * *

From my room in the House Beautiful I had seen some green hills and sparkling rivers. But so far the Way of the King was only taking us through dry, dangerous ground – with no sign of anything green.

We walked on together, talking about the King and his Son. After a time I turned round to see how far we'd come, and noticed someone hurrying towards us.

"It's Evangelist," I shouted in excitement, pleased to see my friend again. I was so grateful that Evangelist had taken the time to talk to me in the City of Destruction, and help me start my journey, but I'd not had a chance to thank him properly.

As Evangelist caught up with us, I told him all the things that had happened to me, including all the mistakes I'd made.

Evangelist smiled. "The King has brought you here safely, Christian, and he will always help you."

"I'm sure he will," I agreed.

Evangelist turned to Faithful. "Tell me about your adventures."

Faithful looked embarrassed, and half-afraid to speak. "I haven't fought any battles yet," he said quietly.

Evangelist obviously knew this. "You love and trust the King with all your heart," he told Faithful. "I'm sure you will be just as brave as Christian if the servants of the evil prince attack you."

Faithful said he hoped he would be.

"Sometimes people have to suffer a lot," Evangelist said. "Remember, Faithful, no matter what happens to you, the King will give you a crown of life."

At the time I wasn't sure what Evangelist was trying to say, but from the quiet look on Faithful's face it seemed he understood the meaning of those words.

"Tell us more about the road," I begged. "Will it be easier now, or are there other frightening places to pass through?"

Evangelist looked serious. "I came to meet you here," he told us, "because you are near the gates of Vanity Fair, a great town that the evil prince built thousands of years ago. It looks like a beautiful place, full of all kinds of pleasant things."

Does Vanity Fair sound like a good place? What do you think Evangelist is going to tell the two pilgrims to do there?

Evangelist explained that there was never a single day when it wasn't possible to find whatever people wanted in the town. "You can buy and sell silver, gold, pearls, precious stones, houses, land, goods, titles, countries, kingdoms and any sorts of pleasure all through the year."

"Do we *have* to pass through it?" Faithful asked, sounding anxious. He'd been extremely quiet since Evangelist mentioned the crown of life.

"The evil prince ordered Vanity Fair to be built across the Way of the King," Evangelist explained. "Every pilgrim going to the Celestial City has to pass through it. Even the King's Son had to pass through there, and the evil prince tried to make him buy some of its goods."

"But we don't have to *stay* there, do we?" I asked, seeing a way out of our problems.

Evangelist shook his head. "No, you don't. But some pilgrims decide to stay for a few days. Then, when they've been in the town a short time, they forget the King."

"What shall we do?" Faithful said. I could tell he was afraid of the place, and I wondered how brave *I* would be if I meet trouble in Vanity Fair.

Evangelist put a hand gently on Faithful's shoulder. "Walk quietly along the streets," he said. "Don't stop to look at the things in the market. Some days the towns-people leave the pilgrims alone, but there are times when they treat them badly."

"Might they even *kill* us?" I asked. It was my turn to sound anxious.

"There have been times when the people have been evil enough to kill people who won't serve their prince,"

Evangelist said. "But don't be afraid, either of you. If you do have to die there, the King will send his angels to carry you to be with him in his City for ever."

The sun was setting by this time, and Evangelist said goodbye. In the fading light we could see the walls and gates of a great town in the distance.

"Are you afraid?" I asked Faithful as we got closer.

"Not very afraid," he said slowly, but I thought he was. "The King will take care of us, and you have your good sword and shield, Christian."

"If you'd stayed at the House Beautiful you would have been given some armour, too," I told him.

"Never mind," Faithful said, with a quick smile. "I'll keep close to you, and if the people *do* kill me, there will be no more enemies to fight."

We passed under the wide archway just as darkness fell, and we heard the heavy gates slam shut behind us.

Someone has jumbled up the letters on this signpost. What is the name of the town?

The next morning we wanted to get through Vanity Fair quickly. As we passed the market in the town square, some small children came running after us, calling us rude names.

The shouting made everyone turn to see what was happening. Even this early in the day, the market stalls had all sorts of bright and shiny goods for sale, but we took no notice. All we wanted to do was get through the town and safely out the other side.

"You need some good clothes," a man shouted from his stall. "Come and look at what I have for sale. You don't need those silly clothes!"

He was talking to me, but I shook my head. "These are the King's clothes," I called out. "We don't need any of your goods. We're going to the Celestial City."

The children were drawing a big crowd by this time, and there was a lot of shouting. One of the evil prince's servants pushed his way towards us through the crowd. He'd probably seen my shining helmet, so he must have known we were pilgrims.

"What are you doing?" he demanded, as he seized us by our shoulders. "Our prince doesn't allow fighting in his streets."

"We're not fighting," I said. "We're walking along quietly."

"That's nonsense," the man shouted. "I've been watching you two boys. You've caused a disturbance here in the market, and you must come with me."

"We're the King's pilgrims," Faithful said confidently. "We're not disturbing anyone. We only want to pass through your town."

"I don't know anything about the King's pilgrims," the man said angrily. "All I can see is that you're two foolish, troublesome young people, and you must be taken before the Governor."

So he led us down the street to the Governor's house, and the people of the town followed, laughing and making fun of us.

The Governor was a nasty man, and he said we must be beaten, then shut in a cage in the market place.

I tried not to cry out as a man beat us on our backs and legs with a long stick, but I think Faithful was braver than me.

The Governor's soldiers bound our hands and feet with chains, threw us into the cage and left us there. I think everyone in the town came to see us. Some people tried to make us say unpleasant things about the King's Son, but we knew that he was with us, even though we couldn't see him.

Someone shouted that we should be allowed to go free, because we were so brave. Someone else shouted that we should stay in the cage for ever, because we were the King's pilgrims.

And then a fight started in the crowd.

What are the people fighting about?

The people are fighting about whether Christian and Faithful have been punished enough, and should be let out.

The next morning, a man came to unlock the door of the cage.

"Are you letting us go free?" I asked, hopefully.

The man laughed. "Free? You're going to the Governor's Court. Judge Hate-Good sits specially to try prisoners like you. You two are in serous trouble. The judge hates the King."

He pulled us out, and we stumbled forward to the courtroom with our legs still in chains. Once there, Judge Hate-Good demanded to know what we'd been doing.

Before I could say anything, two men stood up and told Judge Hate-Good they were afraid we'd do great harm to the young people of Vanity Fair if we were set free. They said they saw us laughing at the treasures with which the prince had filled the town, and pretending we knew of a finer city, and another King whose laws were better than those of their prince.

Judge Hate-Good said we were guilty and must be punished. I looked around in alarm as some soldiers took us from the courtroom, back to the market square.

We were beaten again, and Faithful fell to the ground. Some of the soldiers kicked him hard where he lay. And they keep kicking and beating him.

I looked up, and there in the sky, high above the angry crowd, I could see a chariot and horses. With a sound of trumpets, Faithful was carried up through the clouds by some of the King's special angels, leaving his broken body in the marketplace.

Where has Faithful gone?

Faithful was now living with the King in the Celestial City, but I woke up not having any idea where I was. I felt too weak to open my eyes and look, but I managed to open them in the end, and realized I was no longer in the cage, but in a small room lying on a low bed.

A woman was bending over me. Although she didn't appear unkind, her face had a strange look that made me careful.

"My husband is the man who keeps the jail," she said. "When you fainted, the soldiers carried you from the marketplace, and I felt sorry for you."

She fetched a bowl of water, and bathed my hands and face, staying with me until I began to feel better.

"You're too young to be a pilgrim," she told me. "I want to keep you here in this house and take care of you."

That was when I knew I'd been right to be careful. This woman was planning to stop me going on with my journey.

"I was a pilgrim once," she told me, rather sadly, "but the Way was hard. Anyway, I've been happy enough in this town."

"You'd be happier with the King," I said. "Faithful is with him already. I saw the King's angels waiting for him. And if the Governor ever lets me out of this place, I'm going to travel as fast as I can to the end of my journey."

The woman bent down closely, and I could see unhappiness in her eyes. "I was sorry when they told me about Faithful," she whispered, "but they're not going to kill you."

"I don't think I'd mind if they do," I said. "I'll go straight to the Celestial City. Now it seems I'll be kept here forever."

"If you stay here in Vanity Fair with me, I promise I'll be kind to you," the woman told me.

I shook my head. "I can't stay. I love the King, and I must go to him as soon as they let me out of here."

Four days later the keeper of the jail told me that the governor of the town had given an order for me to be given my armour and set free.

The jailor's wife said she was sorry to see me go, and as I left she told me to think of her sometimes.

"I'll let the King know you've helped me," I promised. "Perhaps you'll be a pilgrim again some day. If I see you coming into the Celestial City I'll recognize you."

The woman said nothing as I walked away quietly down the street. I wasn't feeling strong enough to walk quickly, and I was afraid the people would run after me and hurt me again.

I was just passing through the great archway of the far town gate, when I felt a hand on my shoulder!

Oh dear, is Christian in trouble again?

The boy who had stopped me looked frightened. "Let me come with you, Christian," he said in a half whisper. "I don't want to stay in Vanity Fair any longer."

"Are you a pilgrim too?" I asked in surprise.

"I used to be one. My name is Hopeful, and I hate this place. I've stayed here too long, and I want to be a loyal pilgrim again."

When we were clear of the town, Hopeful looked round anxiously. Seeing no one was close, he said, "Some of us were sorry when they killed Faithful. He was brave, and I'm sure he was good. I was passing the jailor's house when they let you go. You don't mind me coming, do you?"

"Not if you really love the King," I told him. "I was thinking I'd have to go the rest of the way by myself, so I'm glad to have company."

"I wanted you to say that," Hopeful said. "I always meant to run away some day."

Before long we came to an open field where the pathway was smooth and easy. Something to the side caught our attention, and we turned to look. It was a dark opening in the hill, like the mouth of a cave.

A boy stood on the hill, calling to us. "My name is Demas. Come up and see this."

"What is it?" I asked.

"It's a silver mine, and some people are already digging in it for treasure. With a little work, you may become rich."

"Come on," Hopeful said, "let's go and look."

I had to pull Hopeful back. "No, it's not safe. I think

Demas is a servant of the evil prince. Why else would he invite people to help themselves to silver?"

I called to Demas and asked him if the mine was dangerous.

"It's safe, unless you're careless," Demas shouted back, but even from this distance I could seem him turning red.

"We could go up and have a quick look," Hopeful said in excitement.

"I don't think there's any silver in that mine," I said. "I think there's _ _ _ _ _ _ there instead."

Demas wants to help them,
And that sounds good to me;
Nothing could be better than
Getting silver free;
Everybody does it, so
Run up there and see!

Only read the first letter of each line to find the missing word.

I pulled him away. "Come on, Hopeful, I'm sure I've heard about the **danger** of this place. Anyway, we can't get to it without leaving the path."

"Don't worry," Demas called. "I can see four others coming behind you."

We turned round and saw four boys following us, so we stayed to see what they would do. The four hurried up the hill and into the cave, and I wondered if they would ever come out.

* * *

It was getting dark as we came to the bank of a broad river. A sign said it was the River of the Water of Life, where pilgrims could rest safely. It seemed a good place to stay, so we drank some cool clear water from the river, which was pleasant and made us feel less tired.

Hopeful reached up for some fruit growing from one of the green trees, and I picked a handful of the leaves and rubbed them gently into the wounds where I'd been beaten in Vanity Fair. Immediately I could feel the juice from the leaves soothing my cuts and bruises.

On each side of the river we saw a meadow covered in wild flowers. Everything felt peaceful, so we lay down and soon fell asleep.

When we woke the next morning, we watched the sun rise over the hills, and ate more of the fruit and drank from the river. Later that day we bathed in the cool water, and I could feel my whole body being refreshed. So there we rested in perfect safety, eating the fruit, and drinking the healing water of the river.

When we'd been there for several days, I felt fully recovered from my beatings in Vanity Fair. We were ready to continue the journey, but the place was so nice that we decided to stay for a few more days.

"I wonder if we're far from the Celestial City," I said to Hopeful one morning. "Come on, it's long past time we were on our way again."

Hopeful nodded in agreement. "Perhaps after this long rest we'll be able to travel faster than ever," he said, yawning. "But let's not hurry."

The pilgrims had a well-earned rest,
They even wanted more;
But after staying much too long,
Their feet will soon feel _ _ _ _.

What will soon happen to their feet?

I wasn't looking forward to a long walk. We'd rested too long by the River of the Water of Life, and I felt lazy. As soon as we started walking, **my feet felt sore**, and I hoped the path would be smooth and easy.

We travelled slowly along the Way of the King all that day. Our muscles ached from lack of exercise, my legs felt tired and my back hurt.

Late in the afternoon we came to a place where a stile led off into a broad, green meadow. A sign said *By-Path Meadow*. I recognized the name as meaning Two-Path Meadow, so I thought one path was probably just as safe as the other for pilgrims.

Our path leading from the river was rough and stony, and my feet were already covered in blisters.

A hedge divided the meadow from the Way of the King, and I could see a smooth, grassy path running alongside the one we were on.

"Let's walk along this path for a little way," I suggested, turning to Hopeful. "The stones are cutting my feet."

"And mine," Hopeful said, "but I don't think that path is safe."

"Oh, it's all right," I insisted. "Look, it runs close to the hedge. We'll be able to climb back onto the Way of the King whenever we want."

Hopeful looked unhappy. "All right," he said at last, "if you're *sure* it's safe, Christian, I'll go with you."

We climbed over the stile into the meadow, where the grass felt soft to our feet. As it began to get dark, I started to worry.

"I'm sure we're not on the right path," Hopeful said, "but it's too dark now to see anything."

I didn't answer. I knew I'd done wrong in climbing over the stile, and I wondered how I could have been so stupid to think that any path would be safe if it wasn't the Way of the King.

Before I could speak again, heavy drops of rain hit my face. A blinding flash of lightning darted across the sky, followed by a roar of thunder. Then the rain poured in torrents, and the thunder and lightning were worse than anything I'd ever heard or seen before.

"Quick, let's turn round and go back to the stile," I said in panic. "Let me go first, in case we run into more danger."

Imagine you're Hopeful. Would you let Christian lead the way back? Why do you say this?

Hopeful no longer trusted me, and insisted on leading the way back to the stile himself. The heavy rain had already filled the streams that ran through the meadow, flooding the path by the hedge. In places the water was so deep that we could only just keep our footing. I was certain we'd be drowned before we could get back to the Way of the King.

The storm lasted for several hours, and although we struggled on, we found it impossible to make our way back in the darkness. So we sat under some thick bushes close to the hedge, and fell asleep.

* * *

We woke with a fright, as a loud voice shouted, *"What is that I see shining in the bushes?"*

A giant was striding through the long grass of the meadow, and he was coming our way. "Who are you?" the giant called in a deep, booming voice.

The giant had untidy hair and a rough beard, and clothes made of the skins of wild beasts. "What are you two doing on my land?" he demanded.

"We're pilgrims," I said, feeling so afraid I could hardly speak. "And we've lost our way."

"Is that so?" the giant bellowed. "You two are in trouble, and you're coming back with me to my castle!"

He dragged us by our arms across the fields to his house, which had the name Doubting Castle above the massive doorway. Once inside, the giant threw us into a dark, stinking dungeon, and left us there without anything to eat or drink.

Hopeful crept close to me and we sat together. I was

afraid the giant would lock us up for ever, and we'd never reach the Celestial City.

Suddenly we heard a banging on the door of our dungeon, and a woman's voice called loudly, "My name is Diffidence. I am the wife of Giant Despair. My husband tells me he found you sleeping in his meadow. Oh, how pleased I am to know that you're locked securely in here. My husband is coming to beat you without mercy. And then he'll beat you again. Ah, here he is now. My, what a large stick he has to hit you with." And she screeched with laughter.

When he had beaten us almost lifeless, Giant Despair locked us up again in the dark. We felt so bruised from the heavy blows that we lay on the ground twisting and turning in pain.

* * *

Three days later I begged Giant Despair to set us free. This made him so angry that he opened our prison door and rushed at us with his stick. I thought he was going to kill us, but he fell down in a fainting fit and lay on the ground unable to move.

> *The prison door is open wide,*
> *The giant's on the ground;*
> *Whatever they will both do next*
> *They must not make a sound.*

What would you do now? Be careful, don't forget Giant Despair's wife!

Giant Despair's wife was watching from the shadows. She quickly slammed the prison door shut before we could escape.

"You stupid fellow," she shouted at her husband. "You've lost the use of your hands again. I told you not to stay out in the sun too long. I hope you're not going to let these two pilgrims get away. It wouldn't be the first time."

"I just don't understand why they're so brave," Despair said, ignoring his wife.

"Perhaps," Diffidence told him, "they think someone is coming to save them. Or maybe they have a key hidden in their clothes to open the doors when we're not watching. You've often lost prisoners that way."

The giant looked at his wife and grunted. "If those boys had one of the King's keys, they'd have used it by now. But if it keeps you happy, wife, I'll search them in the morning. Now leave me alone. I'm going upstairs to sleep."

It was quiet in Doubting Castle that night. We called to the King's Son, begging him to help us. Of course, we should have done it days ago. We were prisoners in Doubting Castle, and I think Giant Despair's name made us give up, and his wife Diffidence had affected us too. Her name meant Reserved or Timid, and we'd certainly been too timid to approach the King's Son – until now.

"The King's Son will hear us," I said confidently, "even though we can't see him."

I had a sudden thought. It's as though the King's Son was whispering to me, reminding me of something Giant

Despair's wife had said.

"Oh, how stupid I've been," I said quietly. "We've stayed here all these days in this dark, stinking dungeon, when we could have got away. When I was leaving the House Beautiful, Discretion gave me a Key called Promise. I remember seeing these words on it: *'I have come as Light into the world, so that everyone who believes in me will not remain in darkness.'* If we tell the King's Son that we're sorry we took the wrong path, I believe this Key will open every one of the giant's locks and take us out of this prison into the light."

We knelt on the filthy floor and begged the King's Son to forgive us for going the wrong way, and reminded him of his promises on the key.

Hopeful made me jump as he sprung up. "Let's try it," he said. "It's still early, and Despair and his wife may still be asleep."

We felt carefully in the darkness until we found the lock of the dungeon door. I pushed the Key of Promise into it. It turned easily. I could feel my heart beating fast as we stepped over the threshold and listened.

Who wrote the words on the key?

The King's Son had written the words. A dim light shone down the passage, and we found our way to the gate leading into the courtyard. I slid the Key into the next lock, not daring even to whisper.

The Key turned and the gate swung open quietly. I crept through and Hopeful followed. The moon was shining brightly, and only one more door stood between us and the green meadow.

But this last lock was stiff, and although I tried with all my might, I was unable to turn the Key.

"Oh, *do* try harder," Hopeful cried. "We have to escape before the giant hears us."

"I *am* trying," I insisted, "but the lock is stuck."

Hopeful put his hands with mine on the Key of Promise. "I can feel it turning," he said, and in another moment the lock came undone.

We pushed the gate open quickly, but the rusty hinges made such a noise that Giant Despair came running down the stairs. Then, just as he reached the doorway, his stick dropped from his hands, and he fell heavily to the ground.

The sun was just coming up over the horizon as we ran as fast as we could towards the stile that led back to the Way of the King.

We jumped over the stile and sat down by the roadside, still out of breath from running. I felt sure Despair wouldn't follow us now we were no longer on his land.

"Well, I'm glad Discretion gave me the Key," I said, as soon as I thought we were safe.

Hopeful agreed. "I don't think we could have escaped without it."

I nodded. "When I held that Key, I thought of all the promises the King's Son has made. But it's a pity pilgrims don't know where that path leads. Maybe we should write a warning on a stone and set it up near the stile."

"I can do it," Hopeful said, "if we can find a stone."

We look up and down and soon found a large, smooth rock lying in the long grass.

"This will do," I said. "You mark out the letters, Hopeful, and then we'll push it into the right place."

Hopeful found a large iron nail by the stile, and began to carve some words onto the stone.

There are 39 words in Hopeful's sign. Write your own warning on a piece of paper. There don't have to be 39 words in yours, but you should mention Giant Despair, Doubting Castle and the Key of Promise. When you've finished, turn the page and see if your warning is better!

Over this stile is the way to Doubting Castle,
which is kept by Giant Despair.
He despises the King of the Celestial Country,
and seeks to destroy his holy pilgrims.
The Key of Promise opens all the giant's locks.

We pushed the stone across the grass, and placed it close to the stile to By-Path Meadow so that no one could pass by without seeing it.

"It will be sure to save someone," Hopeful said. "I'm glad you thought of it, Christian."

We walked on, slowly and painfully, until we came to a place where some hills rose in front of us.

The hills looked familiar, and then I realized why. "I saw them in the distance, when I was at the House Beautiful," I told Hopeful.

As we came close to the mountains, we found gardens and orchards, and vineyards and fountains of water. So we washed ourselves clean of the filth and smell from Giant Despair's dungeon, then ate some of the fruit and drank clear, fresh water from a spring.

Four shepherds hurried down to greet us. "Welcome to the Delectable Mountains," they said. "This country is called Immanuel's Land. It belongs to the King's Son. You can sometimes see the King's City from the top of these hills."

"Are these his sheep?" I asked, pointing to the flock they were looking after.

"These sheep are here as a picture of the Celestial City, for pilgrims to see," one of the shepherds explained.

"The King's Son has rescued each of these sheep from danger, just as he rescued you. Now he's making sure they are cared for in safety."

"Is the rest of the way to the Celestial City safe?" Hopeful wanted to know.

The shepherd scratched his chin. "It's safe for those who love the King and his Son, but pilgrims who don't serve him faithfully can fall into danger."

The shepherds said their names were Knowledge, Experience, Watchful, and Sincere, and they led us to their tents where they gave us plenty of good, nourishing food.

"I can see how exhausted you are," Watchful said after the meal. "It's late and I think it's time you were both in bed. You can stay with us tonight."

I lay awake in bed, hoping that one day some pilgrims would kill Giant Despair and his wife, and destroy their home. At last the two of us slept comfortably, and woke the next morning feeling much less sore from our beatings in Doubting Castle.

Do you think anyone will kill the giants? If so, who? Think of some people who didn't start the journey with Christian, but you hope will be coming along later.

No answer here. You will have to wait and see if anyone does!

The shepherds wanted to show us some of the special sights on the mountains before we left, so they took us up to the very top of Mount Clear. Even though it was a sunny morning, we could see a light shining in the far distance.

"That's the Celestial City," the shepherd called Sincere told us. "If your eyes are good you may be able to see its Golden Gates."

But the light was brighter than the sun. "I can only see something shining," I said, screwing up my eyes.

"It certainly is too bright for you," Sincere told me, "but we have a telescope called Faith, which will make it seem clearer."

I took the telescope, but I was so excited that my hands shook too much to hold it steady.

Then Hopeful tried. "I think I can see something that looks like dazzling gold."

Experience let us look for some time before taking the telescope back. Then he said it was time for us to continue our journey. "You will soon come to the Enchanted Ground," he warned us. "Take care you don't go to sleep there. The land belongs to the evil prince."

"If I could only have seen the Celestial City," I said to Hopeful as we waved goodbye to the shepherds. "I really wanted to see it."

"Well," Hopeful said, "I'm sure I saw the Gates, so we know it's not far away now."

At the foot of the mountain we came to a twisting lane leading off the Way of the King. The signpost said the lane led to a place called Conceit, and a boy was running from there towards us.

"What sort of place is Conceit?" I asked the boy.

"It's a large town where I live, beyond the hills," the boy told us. "My name is Ignorance and I've decided to go to the Celestial City."

I was wondering why he'd come from the wrong direction. "Do you think they'll let you in?"

"Why not?" he said in surprise. "Surely they let *everybody* in!"

Ignorance is on his way

But there's a problem – wait;

Shouldn't he have started out

At the W _ _ _ _ _ G _ _ _ ?

I shook my head. "We've been sealed by the Spirit of the King on our foreheads, and our Rolls of Faith show that our names are already written in the Celestial City. Did the King give you anything?"

Ignorance smiled. "Of course he didn't, but I can't see it will matter. I've lived a good life and I always try to help people. I even call to the King sometimes. *You* can follow the King in whatever way you like, and *I'll* follow him *my* way. All right? You have *your* faith and I have *mine*. I expect mine is just as good as yours."

"But," I said, "the King's pilgrims have to be welcomed in by his Son at the Wicket Gate, and go past the Cross. The King's Son says he is the only Way to start. Did you do that?"

"You needn't make such a fuss about it," Ignorance snapped. "I don't know where you've come from, but you were probably living near the Wicket Gate, so of course it was easy for you. Nobody in the town of Conceit *ever* thinks of starting there. In fact, I don't believe anybody knows this Wicket Gate you're talking about. We have a gentle pathway that saves us such a lot of trouble, and of course it makes our journey shorter and easier."

I didn't know what to say, as Ignorance stopped to pick some fruit.

Hopeful said, "Shall we wait for him?"

"He's not stupid," I told him. "If Ignorance wants to know about the Way to the King, he'll soon catch us up. I'd like to help him, but we mustn't let him stop us going."

Later in the day we came to a wide plain, between the

Delectable Mountains and a country with low hills and long valleys. A signpost said it was called the Enchanted Ground.

Hopeful yawned. "I'm too tired to go on. Let's lie down and rest."

He certainly sounded ready for sleep. "Not here," I said quickly.

"Why not?" Hopeful asked drowsily. "There's no one to hurt us. You go on. I'll only be a few minutes." And he lay down.

Hopeful is already snoring: zzzzz. Even the question has some snores in it. What does it say?

Is it safe to sleep here? No, it's not!

Hopeful was already sleeping on the grass, but I quickly pulled him up and shook him hard. "What *are* you thinking about?" I said. "Don't you remember the shepherds warned us about the Enchanted Ground? They told us it's not safe to sleep here."

Hopeful was quickly awake. "Sorry," he muttered, "but I don't think I've ever felt so sleepy before. Imagine what would have happened if I'd been on my own. I might never have woken up."

"I'm feeling sleepy, too," I admitted. "Let's hurry on our way and talk about something interesting. You've never told me how you began to be a pilgrim."

"I started out before you did," Hopeful said. "I knew Evangelist well, and he used to tell me about the King. I was living a dishonest sort of life, but I shut my eyes and ears to anything to do with the King and his Son. Then, one day, I decided to do something about it."

"What?" I asked.

"I decided to make my own changes," Hopeful said, as we walked quickly. "I stopped doing and saying bad things, called to the King a bit and that sort of thing. But it didn't make any difference. I knew that inside I was as bad as ever."

"Tell me more," I said.

Hopeful gave an embarrassed smile. "Every time I heard anyone mention the King and his Son, or I heard about someone going to the Celestial City, I thought it was time to start working my way there. But Evangelist told me it was no good trying to get there by pleasing the King. I had to start at the Wicket Gate and go to the Cross – just as I was. So I ran there and began my journey the proper way. When I came to Vanity Fair I thought it was good, and the people persuaded me to stay."

That surprised me, for I'd found the town unpleasant. "You really liked Vanity Fair?"

"Well, I liked it sometimes, but I often felt frightened and unhappy. When pilgrims passed through the town, I was afraid they'd recognize me. Then you came with Faithful, and the minute I saw you both I felt so ashamed."

"Did you see us being beaten?"

"Yes, and I watched you when you were in the cage. Once I crept up close to the bars. I think you were asleep, but Faithful saw me and spoke to me."

"What did he say?"

"He begged me to leave the city at once. He told me the King's Son loves me and would forgive me if I told him I was sorry. I can remember some words Faithful told me, words that he said were spoken by the King's Son."

.em ot semoc ohw enoyna yawa nrut reven lliw I

You have to read the whole sentence backwards, but not in a mirror.

Hopeful told me, "The words were, *'I will never turn away anyone who comes to me.'* Then I saw Faithful killed because he loved the King, and I made up my mind that if you were set free, I'd ask you to let me travel with you."

"I'm glad you did," I said.

Hopeful nodded. "I'm glad too, Christian. Glad the King's Son hasn't turned me away, and glad to know he never will."

Ignorance had been following us off and on for some time.

"He's only a little way behind us now," Hopeful said. "Shall we wait for him?"

I wanted to help Ignorance if I could. "Perhaps it would be better. If he feels sleepy we can at least keep him awake."

We waited, but although Ignorance was able to see us waiting, he took a long time to catch up.

"It's is a pity for you to stay behind," I called to him, as he strolled slowly towards us. "Come on, we can help you start your journey the right way."

Ignorance shrugged. "I'd just as soon walk by myself. I always have so much to think about."

"What do you think about?" Hopeful asked.

"The King and the Celestial City."

"But *thinking* about them isn't enough," I told Ignorance. "The evil prince thinks about them, too – but he's not allowed in."

I noticed Ignorance turning red with anger. "I suppose you think you're so perfect," he snapped.

"No, I don't," I said. "The King's Son is the one who's perfect, and he's promised us a place in his Father's City."

"Perhaps he's promised one to me," Ignorance said.

"Ask him if he has," I suggested.

Ignorance shook his head. "That sort of thing is all too much trouble, if you want to know."

I felt sorry for Ignorance. "We can only get into the City if we've been forgiven," I told him. "No one gets in just by being good."

"We'll see about that," Ignorance said, sitting down angrily on the grass. "I've left my home, and now I'm living like a pilgrim. What else can I do? Anyone would think I wasn't already good enough."

"We can never make ourselves good enough to please the King," I said. "That's why his Son chose to die for us on the Cross. There's a song I know, but I can't remember all of the last line.

"The King was angry with us all,
'I'll punish you,' he said;
But then he took his only Son
And punished him i _ _ _ _ _ _."

"He punished his Son, instead of punishing us for all the things we've done wrong," I told Ignorance, but he still didn't seem to understand.

I turned to Hopeful. "I don't know what else to say," I whispered. "No one is good enough to get into the Celestial City by themselves, but Ignorance won't believe us."

Ignorance was growing tired of talking. "You two have such silly ideas," he sighed. "I don't want to walk with you anymore."

"Come on, Hopeful," I said, "it looks as though we'll be travelling by ourselves again."

We went ahead, and Hopeful shook his head in wonder. "If everyone gets into the Celestial City, why did we have to pass by the Cross and go through all those difficulties?" he asked.

"We'll watch and see what happens to Ignorance at the Dark River," I said. "I think you'll get your answer then."

Hopeful yawned loudly. "Well, I hope we're almost past the Enchanted Ground."

"Are you still tired?"

"A bit, Christian. Perhaps we've been talking too much."

I pointed down the road. "I think we're close to the Land of Beulah."

Hopeful looked brighter when he heard that. "Come on," he said, speeding up, "I can't wait to get there."

It seemed only a short time before we left the Enchanted Ground and entered the country of Beulah. The air was sweet and pleasant, and I was pleased to see that the Way of the King led right into Beulah.

I couldn't remember ever seeing so many flowers before, and hearing so many different birds sing. We were safely past the Dark Valley, out of the reach of Giant Despair, and we certainly couldn't see places like Doubting Castle and Vanity Fair from here.

What we could see was the Celestial City across the Dark River. As I looked at it, knowing it was where the King and his Son lived, I began to feel shaky with joy. I had to sit down to recover, and Hopeful sat with me.

"The thought of what's ahead is almost too much to take in," he said, as his eyes sparkled.

As soon as we were feeling better, we continued on our way, going past orchards, vineyards and gardens. Although they were fenced in, we found open gates to go through. By the edge of a wood we saw a small arbour.

Let me tell you what an arbour is. It's a sort of *reltesh*; I mean a sort of *trelesh*. No, I mean it's a sort of *leshert*. Sorry, I keep mixing up the letters! Can you sort them out and make the right word?

I noticed a man watching us. We told him who we were and he explained he was the gardener.

"Who do all these gardens and orchards belong to?" I asked.

"They are the King's," he said. "He planted them here for his own enjoyment, and also as a place where pilgrims like you can rest."

The gardener invited us to pick fruit and refresh ourselves. "There's a **shelter** here, where you can sleep," he said, showing us the **arbour** built from timber and green leaves.

"Oh, Hopeful," I said one evening, as we sat in the arbour, watching the sun slowly sink behind the hills, "aren't you glad we came? I seem to be forgetting all the troubles we've had, now that we're happy."

Hopeful smiled. "I'm glad I didn't lose my Roll of Faith at Vanity Fair. The King's Son must surely have been helping me."

The gardener came and stood by us. "What happens to pilgrims now?" I asked him.

The man sat down with us and put a hand on his chin, deep in thought. "Some pilgrims live quietly in this land for many years," he said, "but usually the King gives them work to do in the country of the evil prince."

"I remember when Help pulled me out of the Slough of Despond," I told the gardener. "He said he'd been to the Gates of the City, but the King had given him some work to do before he could enter. I'll go away and work for the King if he wants me to, but I think I'd like best to go straight to the City."

Hopeful agreed. "So would I."

The King's gardener told us of the good things that lay ahead. So we stayed happily in Beulah, talking and thinking about the King. A few angels walked with us from time to time, for we were on the border of the Celestial City.

We watched Ignorance walk past the gates of the King's gardens, but he wasn't wearing the King's clothes, and the gardener didn't invite him in. I noticed that the angels, although they saw Ignorance as he walked along, didn't speak to him or give him any encouraging message from the King.

One day we followed Ignorance to the bank of the Dark River. He kept looking across at the walls of the Celestial City, then he stepped into the water. The water was rough and he jumped back out, a puzzled look on his face.

"I don't want to cross just yet," I heard him say.

I hurried over to Ignorance. "It's still not too late to go through the Wicket Gate and find the Cross," I told him. "I know the Way, and I can take you there if you like."

What do you think Ignorance will say?

Ignorance shook his head. "I can't be bothered about that sort of thing now. Anyway, it's probably too late."

Hopeful joined us. "No, it's never too late," he said. "Not until you cross the Dark River."

Ignorance sighed loudly. "That's where I'm going," he said, pointing to the walls of the Celestial City. "I've not been a bad person, so I don't think there'll be a problem. I can't see a bridge, so maybe there's a boat to carry the pilgrims over."

"There *is* a boat," a voice said behind us.

We turned to see who was speaking. It was the King's gardener.

"There *is* a boat," he repeated quietly, out of the hearing of Ignorance, "but it belongs to the evil prince. The King's pilgrims never use it. The boatman's name is Vain-Hope. Here he comes now. Look, he's seen Ignorance, and he's rowing towards him."

"Come on, Ignorance, it's time for you to cross over," the boatman called, as he drew his craft into the river-bank. "I've brought my boat for you."

Ignorance looked pleased. "I suppose the King sent you."

"Of course," Vain-Hope replied, but it sounded like a lie.

He held out his hand and Ignorance took it, stepping into the boat. Then Vain-Hope picked up his oars and prepared to row across the rough water.

"What do I do when I get to the other side," we heard Ignorance ask.

Vain-Hope pointed to a path on the opposite bank.

"That's the best way," he explained. "It's smooth and easy. If the King's angels had come to meet you, they'd have taken you by another road that's steep and difficult to climb. Go straight up to the Golden Gates, and you'll soon find your way to the King's palace."

We watched the boat reach the far bank of the River, where Ignorance got out. He turned and began to climb the path towards the City.

"What will happen to him now?" I asked the gardener.

"Ignorance will come to a gateway," the gardener said. "On the archway he will see some words written in large letters:

"BLESSED ARE THOSE WHO WASH THEIR ROBES,
SO THAT THEY MAY HAVE THE RIGHT
TO THE TREE OF LIFE,
AND MAY ENTER BY THE GATES INTO THE CITY."

The gardener shook his head. "Ignorance will think to himself that he's tried to do his best, so he'll call out, 'I'm a pilgrim, and I've just crossed the River. I wish to live in the Celestial City."

I frowned. "And then?"

The gardener looked unhappy. "Then Ignorance will be asked for his Roll of Faith. I have seen it happen many times. He will put his hand into his pockets and pretend to feel for it."

"Won't he be let in?" Hopeful asked.

"The City is so beautiful," I added. "I want to live there forever."

"And so you will," the gardener assured us. "You came through the Wicket Gate and went past the Cross. The King's own Son built the Wicket Gate, but Ignorance chose not to go through it. So he has no place in the Celestial City."

* * *

I often sat with Hopeful to watch angels from the Celestial City, as they came across to visit the people who lived with us in the land of Beulah. Sometimes they brought messages from the King to his servants, and we learnt that it would not be long before a message was given to us.

One morning, while we were walking slowly among the vines, we saw two angels coming down the path to meet us.

"Are you travelling to the Celestial City?" the angels asked.

"Yes," we replied together.

The angels asked us many questions, and we told them everything that had happened since we began our pilgrimage. I told of my difficulties and dangers, and Hopeful explained how he wasted so much time in Vanity Fair.

"We've often behaved badly," I said, "but we've been sorry afterwards."

"We have," Hopeful added quietly.

"Forgiveness is a gift offered by the King, and you have accepted it," the angels told us.

"We love the King with all our hearts," I said.

"He knows you do," the angels replied. "And he's sent us to tell you he wants you to enter his City."

Hopeful said he felt excited. I wanted to feel like that, but when I thought of meeting the King I became anxious, and said to the angels, "Will you go with us?"

"We will go with you a little way," they promised, "and meet you again at the Gates of the Celestial City."

They told us to follow them, and we went out of the garden and down to the edge of the Dark River. The reflection of the sun shining on the other side was so glorious that we weren't able to see clearly, but the water between us and the Celestial City looked especially dark.

"Oh," I cried, almost in panic, "if we don't use Vain-Hope's boat, how are we to get across?"

They will have to walk through:

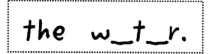

the w_t_r.

"You have to walk through **the water**," the angels said, "but there's no need to be afraid. The King's City is on the other side, and you will soon be safely inside its Gates."

Hopeful raised his head and looked across the river. "Look," he said, "I can see the Gates. Oh, Christian, why are you frightened?

"It's all right for you," I said, "but the King is never going to receive me. I've been a bad pilgrim."

I could no longer see the light beyond the Dark River, and I shivered as I looked at the cold water, then turned once more to the angels. "It's too deep," I said. "I'll be drowned."

"No," the angels told me, "you won't find it too deep. Don't look at the water, Christian, but lift up your eyes to the light."

I tried to be brave. "Do the King's pilgrims always cross safely?"

"Yes, Christian, always," the angels said. "Do not be afraid. Trust in the King, and remember all that he has done for you through his Son."

The angels turned away, and Hopeful put his arm round my shoulders. "Come on, Christian, we'll soon be over. I know the King will take care of us."

We walked slowly down the bank and stepped into the cold River.

I could feel the water pulling at me, trying to drag me under. But Hopeful held me tightly, his eyes fixed on the far bank.

"I keep thinking of all the bad things I've done in my life," I gasped, as a wave hit me in the face. "You go on,

Hopeful. I don't deserve to get across safely."

Hopeful wasn't giving up on me. "I can see people waiting for us on the other side," he said. "Just keep going, Christian. The King loves you and wants you with him."

Then I heard the King's Son calling to me with words I'd read in my Book. "When you pass through the waters, I will be with you."

I felt my courage returning, and I could touch the river bed and walk to the far bank. The two angels who led us down to the Dark River were there to receive us.

The City stood on a great hill, but we went up to it easily because the angels held us by our arms. I looked down at my clothes, wondering if I'd kept them clean enough to meet the King and his Son. To my amazement I saw that we'd been given shining clothes, and far below, floating away in the River, were the ones we'd travelled in.

Suddenly we were swept up by a host of angels telling us about the beauty and joy that we would find in the Holy City.

Can you remember all the words on the archway? Can you remember *some* of them?

I looked at Hopeful, with tears in my eyes. "I want to thank the King and his Son for bringing us safely here," I said.

"And so you shall," the angels told us. "The King's Son will wipe away every tear from your eyes. There will no longer be any death. There will no longer be any sadness, or crying or pain. That is all in the past."

"And what are we to do here?" I asked.

The angels smiled. "You will be able to praise the King with shouting and thanksgiving. You will meet your family and friends who have already crossed the Dark River, and they will welcome you with joy."

We came to an archway, with the words that the gardener told us were written there:

BLESSED ARE THOSE WHO WASH THEIR ROBES,
SO THAT THEY MAY HAVE THE RIGHT
TO THE TREE OF LIFE,
AND MAY ENTER BY THE GATES INTO THE CITY.

The King's servant looked down from the archway, and took our Rolls of Faith to carry to the King. The Rolls were sealed with the King's Son's own seal, and I knew that when the King saw the seal he would be glad.

Sure enough, the servant returned quickly and ordered the Gates to be opened, so he could take us to the King.

We passed through the gateway and found young Faithful and my mother, and a great crowd waiting to receive us with music and songs of welcome. I noticed that Hopeful didn't have any friends to greet him, for he'd left them behind in the City of Destruction. But people gathered round and spoke kindly to him, and he seemed to forget his loneliness at once.

I heard the bells in the City ring again for joy, and the King's Son came to us, and said, "Christian and Hopeful, you are good and faithful servants. Come and share my joy."

The City shone like the sun, and the streets were paved with gold. People walked with crowns on their heads, palms in their hands, and golden harps to sing praises.

Then Hopeful sang, "Blessing and honour and glory and power belong to the One sitting on the throne, and to the Lamb forever and ever."

I knew then why the King's Son is called the Lamb. He let himself be killed as a sacrifice, to take all my guilt and wrongdoing away so I could stand here in front of him, washed clean.

The King's Son held me securely in his arms. "Do not be afraid, Christian," he said. "I am the First and the Last. I am the Living One. I was dead, but now I am alive for ever and ever."

And the angels sang, "Holy, holy, holy is the Lord God Almighty."

I was in Heaven!

PART 2

CHRISTIANA'S STORY

MY NAME IS CHRISTIANA. I think my friend Christian has already told you about me. I expect he said I was too busy at home to join him on his journey to the King. Well, I still am busy, ever so busy, because I have four younger brothers to look after. I expect Christian told you that, too.

I live in a place called the City of Destruction, which is as bad a city to live in as its name sounds. The only place where I feel happy is on the hill above the city, which is where I am now.

I like to sit up high like this. It's where I once sat with Christian – before he went on his journey. I have my four brothers with me today, and they're all younger than me. I'm worried how I'm going to look after them in the coming winter.

I often think about the journey Christian made, and wonder where he's living. Is he in the Celestial City, or was he lost crossing the Dark River?

While my mother and father were travelling to the Celestial City they begged me to start my journey – and take my brothers with me. Then last year my father entered the Dark River. A few days later, my mother followed him.

Christian often talked about a special Book he was

reading, but I didn't really believe what the Book said.

I look across the open fields and see a light shining brightly in the distance. I remember Christian telling me there's a high wall there, and a door in it with a Wicket Gate where pilgrims must start their journey.

Perhaps we'll all go there one day. Matthew and Samuel are probably old enough, but as I look at Joseph and James who are eight and nine, and they do seem rather young. I think I'll have to wait a couple of years, because I can't leave them behind.

I stand up and signal to my brothers to follow me back to our home in the City of Destruction.

Joseph and James are aged 8 and 9. Are they old enough to start out on the journey that Christian has already taken? If not, how old do you think they need to be?

You will have to read a few more pages before you find the answer!

It's the evening now, and I've prepared tea for my brothers, which went down well. The four of them are out in the streets with their friends, and the house is quiet. I sit by the fire and keep thinking about our father and mother – and about Christian.

In the night I have a lovely dream. I'm in the Celestial City, walking along its streets with Christian. My brothers are there with us. We go into a wonderful palace where the King's Son meets us and speaks to us.

I wake up with a jump. I wish it had been true, and not just a dream. Although it's early, I get dressed and begin to tidy the house. After breakfast, I jump as someone knocks on the door.

I expect to see a neighbor, but a woman visiting the city is standing there. She says her name is Wisdom, and she's the daughter of Evangelist.

"Christiana, I've wanted to speak to you for some time," Wisdom says, "but I've not been able to find you in the streets."

"No," I say, "I'm tired of the city, so I usually go up the hill to get away from it."

Wisdom lays her hand on my shoulder. "I don't think you're all that happy."

"I'm not," I tell her. "I'm lonely."

"Why is that? You have your brothers."

"I'm lonely because our father and mother have crossed the Dark River, and so has Christian, and I don't know what's become of them."

"They're with the King in his wonderful City. That's why the King's Son has sent me to tell you to start your journey at once."

I shake my head. "My brothers . . ."

"You must bring them with you," Wisdom says quickly. "The King's Son will take care of you all."

"So many of us?" I can't believe what I'm hearing. I wonder if the King knows what my brothers are like. I wonder if he knows what *I'm* like.

Wisdom smiles. "The King's City is large, and there's room in it for every pilgrim." She draws out a folded sheet paper.

"What is it?" I ask.

"It's a letter from the King. Keep it safe and read it often."

"What does it say?" I have to know, but my eyes are running too much to see it clearly.

"It's a promise from the King. To you."

"For me?" I turn away to hide my tears. Not only is Wisdom being kind, but the King has even sent me a letter.

Christiana's tears have smudged the paper, making some letters look like an X. Where is she invited to go?

To txe Xelxsxixl Xixy

I'm going **to the Celestial City**, and I'm still finding it hard to believe that the letter is for me. As I read it, my heart fills with joy mixed with unhappiness – joy that the King should send me such a loving message, and unhappiness that I've never even bothered with him before.

I look up again at Wisdom, who is standing near me. "I'll go," I say, "and I'll try to get my brothers to go with me."

Wisdom smiles. "I'm glad," she says. "Don't wait any longer, Christiana. The way is easier for young people, and the King will help you in your difficulties."

"Difficulties?" I'm not sure I want too many difficulties. "Can you go with us? I won't be frightened if you show us the way."

Wisdom shakes her head. "No, Christiana, I have other work to do. But there's no need to be frightened. The King's Son will watch over you. Did you see a light in the distance, when you were on the hill?"

I nod my head. "I've often seen it."

"That light marks the path you must take to the Wicket Gate."

Wisdom leaves me, and I keep reading the letter. In the evening I show it to Matthew and Samuel, the oldest two of my four brothers. "What do you think?" I ask.

"I think you ought to go," Samuel says. Although he's the second oldest, I always think of him as being the most sensible brother I have.

"I'd like to go, but what will happen to you boys if I leave you alone?" I ask.

"We'll go with you," Matthew, the oldest of the four

says immediately. "At any rate *I* will."

"Will you really?" I give him a hug. Matthew is only a year younger than me, but he's not as thoughtful as Samuel.

"I've often thought about going," Matthew tells me. "You know, since our father and mother crossed the Dark River. It will be good for us all to go together."

I smile as I look into the fire. "Our parents will certainly be pleased to see us. But I don't know what to do about Joseph and James. James is probably too young for such an adventure."

The door flies open, and my two youngest brothers rush in. "What are you three talking about?" James, the youngest, asks.

"Christiana has a letter," Samuel tells him, as he puts it on the table where both brothers can read it.

"**Look, it's from the King,**" Joseph says excitedly. "Why has he written to Christiana?"

"Who brought it?" James asks. "Did it *really* come from the King?"

"One of the visitors to the city brought it," I explain. "Her name is Wisdom. I'm sure you've seen her in the streets."

"She spoke to me the other day," Joseph says, "and I liked her. So are you going?" He comes round to the fire and leans against my chair, looking into my face.

"If I do, will you come with me, Joseph?" I ask.

"I don't mind. Will we have to fight anybody? Are there any wild beasts?"

"I don't know, but Wisdom says the King's Son will watch over us. We have to pass through a Wicket Gate with the light over it. Do you remember hearing how Pliable went with Christian, and both of them fell into the Slough of Despond."

"That terrible place?" Joseph pulls a face.

"What is it?" James asks.

"It's a great bog like quicksand that sucks people down," Joseph says, and he makes a loud sucking noise as he tries to frighten his younger brother.

"Then *we'll* be careful," Samuel says. Yes, he's by far the most sensible of all my brothers, and I think he's also the bravest.

"I'd like to be a pilgrim, Christiana," Joseph tells me, jumping up and down, "but what about James? You can't leave *him* behind."

"No," I tell him, "of course we can't." I have to smile,

for Joseph is only a year older than James. If Joseph can make it, surely James can too.

"Does that mean we're all going?" Joseph asks. "Please say we are, Christiana. Please."

I nod happily. "If that's what you want."

"When can we start? Tomorrow?" Joseph is still jumping up and down.

I want to jump up and down too, but as their sister I have to behave a little more sensibly. "The next day, I think. We can prepare everything at night and leave early, as soon as the gates of our city are opened."

On a piece of paper, write down the names of Christiana and her four brothers, starting with the oldest and finishing with the youngest.

Christiana, Matthew, Samuel, Joseph and James.

This will be my last afternoon in the City of Destruction, and one of my friends has called to see me. Her name is Mercy. She's the same age as Matthew. Unfortunately, Mercy's mother has come as well. We call Mercy's mother Mrs. Bats-Eyes, but of course not in front of her. James thought of the name last year, and I told him it's extremely rude to make up names for people. But we all use it now. I don't think Mercy knows it's what we call her mother. At least, I hope she doesn't.

Mrs. Bats-Eyes has a habit of saying, "I can't see this, I can't see that," whenever anyone has an idea she doesn't agree with. She has a friend we call Mrs. Know-Nothing, and I'm glad to say she hasn't come this afternoon.

"Oh, you *do* look busy, Christiana," Mrs. Bats-Eyes says. "We're here to invite you to go with us to the country tomorrow."

"I don't think I can," I say, not wanting to say too much about my plans. "I have so many things to do at the moment."

"I can't see that matters. Not if you want to be with Mercy," Mrs. Bats-Eyes says. "No, I can't see it at all."

I'm glad my brothers are out. They would all be looking at each other and giggling by now.

"You're packing everything away," Mercy says. "Are you getting ready for a journey, Christiana?"

I've not planned to tell Mercy about the King's letter, but now I feel it would be better to say what I'm going to do.

"I've received a message from the King," I say, "and I'm going to the Celestial City."

"Oh," Mrs. Bats-Eyes cries, "I can't see that's a sensible thing to do at all."

"I'd like you to come with me, Mercy," I say, avoiding her mother's eyes.

"And leave this beautiful city and all her friends?" Mrs. Bats-Eyes gives a loud snort. "I can't see why Mercy would want to do that, Christiana. And what will your brothers do? It's wrong of you to think of leaving them."

"I'm not leaving them. They're coming with me."

Mrs. Bats-Eyes laughs. "You must be mad, girl. How can young boys like Joseph and James be pilgrims? We all know about your friend Christian and his troubles. He was nearly lost in the Slough of Despond. How do you think that place got its name?"

"Because it's like a marsh," I say, worried now that Mercy's mother might talk me out of going.

When Christian got stuck in the marsh, he had someone with him who was stuck as well. Who was it?

You may need a mirror to read this name.

"The Slough of … *Despond.*" Mrs. Bats-Eyes says the last word loudly. "It sucks people under. **Pliable was stuck** there, as well as Christian. No, I really can't see it's a good idea."

"I've made my mind up to go," I say firmly.

Mrs. Bats-Eyes hasn't finished. "Two boys told us that Christian met *lions* on Hill Difficulty."

"I'm not afraid of lions," I say, but of course I am.

"Yes," Mrs. Bats-Eyes continues, "and you can't have forgotten the news from Vanity Fair about young Faithful. You're stupid to run into such danger, Christiana – especially with four brothers who need you to take care of them."

"Matthew's big enough now to take care of *me*," I tell her. "Anyway, the King has promised to watch over us. Look, here's his letter. You can read it if you like."

But Mrs. Bats-Eyes won't even look at it, so I pass it to Mercy.

Mrs. Bats-Eyes stands up. "It's no use wasting our time here," she tells Mercy. "You can go if you want, Christiana, but you'll soon be back!"

I'm not sorry when the door closes and I'm alone again. But only for a moment, for Joseph and James burst in and ask me if anything's the matter.

I tell them how Mercy's mother has been doing her best to talk us out of going to the Celestial City, and they're not to take any notice of my tears.

"Mrs. Bats-Eyes is silly," Joseph says. "She can never see the sense in anything."

"I'm not taking any notice of her," I say, "but I'm glad

Wisdom came here and spoke to me. If she hadn't, I don't think I'd be bothering to pack."

Samuel comes back for tea much sooner than usual, to ask if he can help, eager for us to start our pilgrimage. Matthew, of course, is the last to return. He can be so irresponsible at times.

"I've washed and mended your clothes," I tell my brothers, "but they're getting very shabby. You'll have to look after them carefully."

"Perhaps the King will send us some new ones," Samuel suggests.

"Perhaps he will," I say, but I don't think it's likely.

"Maybe without new clothes we won't be allowed to see the King," James says.

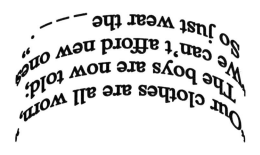

Mercy and her brothers cannot afford new clothes, so what will they have to wear? Will they be allowed into the Celestial City?

Very early in the morning we creep away from our cottage **in our old clothes**, and out through the gates of the city. Joseph and James run on in front because they're anxious to get to the Wicket Gate first.

"Maybe we'll meet a lion," Joseph calls back. "If we do, *I* won't be frightened."

"Nor will I," James adds, sounding fearless. "Pilgrims are *always* brave, and we must fight for Christiana."

I think it's more likely I'll be fighting for them – with the help of Matthew and Samuel, of course. I hear a shout, and turn to see Mercy running across the meadow.

"*Stop!*" she cries. "*Please* let me speak to you, Christiana."

Mercy sounds out of breath as she catches hold of my hand. "Can I walk a little way with you?" she asks.

"You can travel with us all the way to the Celestial City," I tell her.

Mercy shakes her head. "I can't," she says. "The King hasn't sent me a message. I don't think he'll let me into his City if he hasn't invited me."

"I'll tell you what we'll do," I say, having a sudden idea. "Come with us as far as the Wicket Gate, and we'll ask if it's all right for you to pass through."

We go on together happily until we reach the edge of the Slough of Despond, a large soggy marsh.

This is the place where I heard that Pliable and Christian were nearly sucked under and drowned, which makes me more than a little scared – not that I'm going to tell the others. I say, "I don't know how we can get across. It seems rather dangerous."

The soft mud oozes out between the tufts of grass as we move our feet, but as we look around we catch sight of some stepping-stones. Samuel, the bravest, goes first, slowly checking that each stone is firm. Joseph and James follow him, skipping lightly from stone to stone, and we soon find ourselves on the far side on firm ground.

"I want everyone to keep going towards the light," I tell them. "Perhaps we can rest once we've gone through the Wicket Gate."

Who keeps the Wicket Gate?

Turn the page upside down and use a mirror.

About the middle of the day, the six of us reach a large door set into a high wall. Over the door I see the words: *Knock, and the door will be opened to you.* The bright light we saw in the distance shines out from these words that the King's Son has put there.

"You're older than us," Matthew says to me, looking a little scared, "so you'd better be the one to knock."

I lift a small hammer that's hanging by the door and knock, but no one answers. A dog starts to bark somewhere behind us, and although I'm sure Joseph and James mean to be brave, they both turn pale, and whisper, "Can we go home?"

"There's nothing to be afraid of," Mercy says firmly, but I think she's as frightened as my youngest two brothers.

"Knock again," Samuel suggests, standing back with Matthew. "Knock louder this time."

So I lift the hammer and start knocking as hard as I can.

Suddenly a small door within the large one opens. This small door, I realize, is the Wicket Gate. Surely no one could open the large door, but this one is just big enough to let us through one at a time.

"My name is **Goodwill**," a pleasant man says. "Who are you?"

The dog hears his voice and leaves off barking.

"We've come from the City of Destruction where Christian lived," I tell Goodwill, feeling a little braver now that I've seen him smile. "We want to be the King's pilgrims – if you'll let us pass through your door. These are my brothers."

Goodwill leads us through, saying, "I always let young people come to me."

I've seen words like these written in the Book Christian was so fond of reading, and know the King's Son himself spoke them. Just for a moment I wonder if Goodwill *is* the King's Son. Certainly, I could never want to be welcomed by anyone kinder. I smile with relief as I enter the Way of the King, with my brothers following one by one. The Wicket Gate closes behind us.

Suddenly a trumpet sounds out from high on the wall. Goodwill has told a man to play a tune of welcome to five new pilgrims. Five? There should be six of us. I can see my four brothers, so who is missing?

Someone is knocking frantically.

"Don't forget me," I hear a voice call from outside the Wicket Gate, as the trumpeter finishes his piece.

"Is that your friend?" Goodwill asks.

It certainly sounds like her. "I think so," I say.

Goodwill throws the door open. "Are you all right?" he asks.

Mercy is lying on the ground. I think she's fainted with shock at the thought of being shut outside.

Goodwill stoops down and picks her up in his arms. "Don't be frightened," he says softly, as Mercy opens her eyes. "Tell me why you've come."

Mercy looks pale. "I don't have a letter. I only came this far because my friend Christiana let me."

"Did Christiana invite you to go to the Celestial City with her?" Goodwill asks.

"Yes, and I'd like to go. Will the King be angry with me?"

Goodwill shakes his head. "My Gate is open to *everyone* who knocks at it. Didn't you see the promise written above it?"

Mercy nods.

"And can you remember what it says?"

Mercy smiles up at him. "It says, 'Knock, and the door will be opened to you.' That's why I kept knocking."

"I put those words there specially for you," Goodwill tells her. "So of course you can come in."

Goodwill carries Mercy through the Wicket Gate to join us, then leads the way into a cool, quiet room where he says we can rest until he comes for us later.

As soon as we're alone, Mercy says, "It was awful when you'd all gone in, and I was left behind." She's laughing now. Perhaps it's relief. "I didn't like to knock again, until I looked up and saw the words carved over the Gateway. Then I knocked as loudly as I could."

"Loudly?" I say. "I never heard such knocking in all my life. I thought you were going to break the door down!"

"Well," Mercy says, "I couldn't help it. The Wicket Gate was shut, and that fierce dog must have been somewhere near. *You'd* have knocked loudly if you'd felt so frightened."

"I wonder why Goodwill keeps that noisy dog," I say. "But we're all safe now."

Joseph says, "James is afraid it will bite us when we leave here."

I have to smile. It's probably Joseph who's afraid, although he won't admit it. But maybe I'm a bit frightened myself. Perhaps we all are.

James pulls me to one side. "I like Goodwill," he says. "Do you think he's the King's Son?"

What did Goodwill tell Christian?

You'll have to look back to page 13 for the answer.

I don't laugh, which is probably what James is expecting me to do. I've been wondering the same thing ever since we came here.

When Goodwill returns, I'm about to ask him who he really is, when Mercy wants to know why he keeps the dog.

"It's not mine," he says. "There's a dark palace not far from the Wicket Gate. The dog belongs to the evil prince. It lives at the palace, but it can run along his master's land until it comes close to my cottage. Then, as soon as it hears pilgrims knocking, it begins to bark. The evil prince has taught it to do this, but I always open the Wicket Gate as soon as I know someone really wants to come in."

I ask Goodwill about the Way of the King, and he's ready to answer all my questions.

"Before it gets dark you will come to the house of Interpreter," he says. "Knock on the door. It's safe to stop there for the night."

Afterwards he tells us to wash while he prepares a midday meal for us. At last we feel refreshed, and are able to go on our journey.

As we stand outside his house, Goodwill points to a high wall by the side of the road, and says it stops the savage dog seeing us.

The branches of some trees hang over the wall, making a pleasant shade from the sun. Some of the trees are full of ripe berries. As the branches are within easy reach, my brothers of course begin to pick the fruit.

"You shouldn't do that," I warn them. "It may be

dangerous to eat. That garden belongs to the evil prince."

My brothers already have their mouths full. "This fruit is lovely," Matthew says.

Joseph and James are wise enough to listen. They quickly spit their berries out and throw the rest away. I think Samuel has already eaten some, but he stops immediately.

"I'm as big as you," Matthew tells me. "And I know just as much as you do. This fruit is good." So he goes on eating.

Do you think it's safe to eat the berries? They are:

I tell my brothers to behave themselves and keep close to me from now on. Samuel soon feels well again, and Matthew has at last stopped eating the fruit. Joseph and James are keeping much closer to me than they did in the morning, while Mercy says her feet are hurting.

We see a large house in the distance, close to the road. "That must be the house of Interpreter," I tell the others brightly, hoping to make them feel better. "Goodwill said we can sleep there tonight."

The windows are wide open, and as we come up the pathway to the door of the house, we can hear people talking. I knock on the door and a young servant comes to open it.

"Who do you wish to see?" she asks pleasantly.

My brothers and Mercy stand back. I seem to be the one who has to do all the talking when we meet people. "My name is Christiana. I think a friend of mine called Christian stayed here when he was a pilgrim. These are my four brothers, and this is our friend, Mercy."

The young servant goes quickly to a large room where we can see a man sitting at a table with some very young pilgrims who are probably his children. "Can you guess who is at the door?" I hear her say. "It's Christiana, with her brothers and a friend."

The man pushes his chair back and hurries to the door to welcome us. "Come in, come in. My name is Interpreter. Are you really Christiana?" he asks. "Christian told us about you when he came here, and we heard you were on your way."

"Yes, I'm Christiana," I say, feeling embarrassed, and

we all stay on the doorstep. I wish now that I'd started the journey with Christian, because it seems that all the good things he told me are true.

"How pleased Christian will be when he meets you in the Celestial City," Interpreter says. "But we mustn't let you stand at the door. Come in and rest."

Interpreter tells us there are older pilgrims staying in the house, as well as his own family. He takes us into the large hall where everyone is sitting at a long table. They all seem pleased to see us, and two of the women stand up and give Mercy and me a kiss. They give Joseph and James a quick kiss too. The boys are too polite to push the women away, but Joseph wipes his face hard afterwards. Matthew and Samuel must have guessed what is about to happen, and have gone to look out of the window.

I know that an interpreter is someone who explains foreign languages and puzzling things that we can't understand, and wonder what Interpreter is going to explain to us in this house.

After showing them a picture of the Good Shepherd, Interpreter will take Christiana and the others into a room where this man is raking up old straw and dirt.

Interpreter will ask them to look again, and this is what they see. Why doesn't the man look up? Don't turn the page yet. What do you think is happening?

We've been resting for a short time, and now Interpreter is taking us to see a painting of the Good Shepherd. James seems to understand how the sheep in the picture was lost on the mountains, and in great trouble until the Good Shepherd found it and took it in his arms. We all stare at the painting, and it slowly dawns on us that this is the King's Son – and he looks exactly like Goodwill!

Interpreter takes us on to a poorly lit room where a miserable-looking man is working hard. The floor of the room is covered with straw, small sticks and dust. He is holding a rake and using it to pull the rubbish into a heap. He doesn't look up when Interpreter opens the door, and he only seems interested in the rubbish.

"Why is he doing this?" Matthew asks.

"This man keeps asking the King for riches, and now he believes all this rubbish is extremely valuable," Interpreter tells Matthew, although all of us are listening to the answer. "The King is sorry for him, and every day he sends a messenger offering him a golden crown instead of the straw."

We raise our heads and notice an angel holding a bright crown.

"But he doesn't see it," Mercy says, frowning.

"No," Interpreter says. "That's because he won't look up."

I have to swallow hard. "I was just like him," I say. "I always wanted things, and didn't care about the King and his City. But I *do* care now."

I think this man is why Christian's father didn't start the journey with Christian, because he was too busy making money at work. Perhaps he's already started now. I hope he has.

James is wriggling around. "Will the man *never* look up?" he asks.

"I cannot tell you," Interpreter says. "The King is patient, but the man is so sure he'll find treasure in the rubbish, that I don't know if he will ever see the crown."

Interpreter takes us next into a magnificent room and asks what we can see in it. I wonder if this a trick question, because the room is completely empty – apart from a large spider dangling from the ceiling. I don't know what to say.

"I can see a spider," Joseph says. "A great big one."

I tell him not to be so rude.

"Only one spider?" Interpreter asks. "I can see seven." And he's looking at each of us in turn.

What does he mean? There are six of us, which makes seven if he's counting the spider as well. "Do we all look as ugly as the spider?" I ask, rather annoyed with Interpreter. But before he can answer, I understand what he's saying.

Why are we like this spider?

Think of a spider's mouth, and what it uses it for.

"That spider has a nasty bite," I say, "and we sometimes say unpleasant things with our mouths. Am I right?"

Interpreter smiles. "You're very quick," he says.

I'm ashamed of things I've said in the past, and hide my face with my hands. Mercy is blushing, and my brothers have covered their faces. They obviously feel as I do.

"There is still something you have not understood about the spider," Interpreter says with a smile. "This is a fine room, perhaps the finest in the house."

I was about to ask why such a magnificent room has a spider in it, but I didn't want to sound impolite.

We all shake our heads, and Interpreter says, "You may be thinking that the spider doesn't deserve to be here, but we allow it to spin its web. So, even though you often do wrong things, the King will give you a wonderful place in the Celestial City – because you belong to him."

I start to cry when I realize how kind the King is, and I think Mercy is crying too. I'm not sure about my brothers, for they have turned away.

* * *

The next morning we take it in turns to have a bath in wonderful, pure water, and we come out feeling cleaner than we've ever felt before. We feel clean inside and outside.

Interpreter calls us to see him. "The clothes you are wearing are no good for travelling," he tells us. "We must give you some new ones."

"I'm ever so sorry," I say. "I washed and mended them as well as I could, but they're badly worn and I couldn't make new ones in time."

"You did your best," Interpreter tells me, "but even if they *were* new and clean, they would not be suitable. The King's Son has provided clothes for all his pilgrims, and the King will not welcome you in any others."

Mercy and the boys now receive clothes that are spotless. Interpreter also has a set for me.

I look at my brothers and at Mercy, and when I see how good our clothes are, I feel almost frightened. "If the journey is long and difficult," I say to them, "how can we possibly keep these clothes clean until we reach the Gates of the City?"

Joseph and James stand still. "We can never play any more," they say to each other in dismay.

Interpreter smiles and draws the boys nearer to him. "Do not be afraid," he says. "The King loves to see his pilgrims happy. Run about as much as you like, as long as you do not leave the Way of the King."

Do you remember the question about clothes, on page 91? Why can't we stand in front of the King in our own clothes, no matter how new and clean we think they are?

Think what happened to Ignorance, even though he thought he'd done his best.

I look at Mercy. "The King is so good," I tell her. "None of us stands a chance of getting to see him in our own clothes."

Mercy shakes her head slowly in disbelief. "I know I'm a true pilgrim now," she says, with tears in her eyes. "All this time I've been afraid, because I entered the Wicket Gate without getting a message from the King. But now look at me. Oh, the King is so good to me, I could cry for joy."

"You *are* crying for joy," I say, giving her a hug.

"You are washed clean," Interpreter says, "and clothed with righteousness from the King's Son."

Interpreter gives each of us a piece of rolled up paper. "These are your Rolls of Faith," he explains. "You must look after them carefully, because you will need to show them at the Celestial City. You are in the King's family, and are his forever."

Interpreter calls one of his young servants whose name is Greatheart, and says to him, "I want you to go with these pilgrims to the House Beautiful, and keep them safe on the Way."

Greatheart is a tall young man. He's wearing a suit of bright armour and carries a sword at his side. I feel sure he'll be able to protect us if we meet with any danger.

Interpreter and his family give us some food for the journey, and something to drink, and come to the door to watch us set off. Greatheart leads the way, while Joseph and James stay close behind him. I'm walking with Mercy and Samuel, and some way behind us is Matthew.

I turn to see why he's dropping back. "Is anything

wrong?" I call.

Matthew shakes his head.

"Well, you're looking sick." A sudden thought occurs to me. "Are you feeling ill?"

"I don't think so," Matthew says.

"Don't think so, indeed," I say. "Well, I hope it isn't far to the House Beautiful."

"So do I," Matthew says, holding his stomach and dropping even further back.

Why is Matthew holding his stomach?

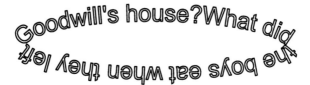

Goodwill's house? What did the boys eat when they left

We've only been going for a short time, and already we've come to the Cross on a small hill. Greatheart says we can stop here for a rest. We sit on the grass and Greatheart tells us how Christian's burden fell from his shoulders when he got here.

"Christian was forgiven by the King's Son when he entered the Wicket Gate," Greatheart explains, "but he still felt the burden of all the things he'd done wrong in the past. But when he came here to the Cross he understood that the King's Son had taken everything from him, so he need not feel guilty any longer."

"When do we see the King's Son?" I ask.

"Didn't you recognize him when he let you through the Wicket Gate?" Greatheart says.

I almost jump with surprise. "The only person we saw was Goodwill." But I remember how James asked me if Goodwill was the King's Son. I'd even been going to put the question to Goodwill, but Mercy asked him about the dog and it went out of my mind.

Greatheart smiles. "Who else do you think could let you into the Way of the King, but the King's Son?"

"But I didn't ..." I start to say.

"You didn't thank him enough." Greatheart finishes the sentence for me. "Don't worry, Christiana, the King's Son knows all about you and he loves you. It is he who has forgiven you for all the things you have ever done wrong, and it is he who has washed you clean, and it is he who will receive you into his Father's City."

"Why is there a Cross?" Joseph asks.

"A good question, Joseph, and one that not everybody understands," Greatheart says. "The King was once angry with every person in the City of Destruction, and he wanted to punish them for doing wrong. But his Son has taken the terrible punishment instead, on this Cross. So now the King can forgive everyone who asks."

To think we actually saw the King's Son when we entered the Way of the King, and didn't realize it. Well, I believe James did. I keep thinking back to the time at the Wicket Gate, wanting to see Goodwill again, so I can remember him more clearly.

"What are those pieces of paper?" I ask, noticing things nailed to the Cross.

"They are lists of all the things each one of you has ever done wrong," Greatheart says. "Why don't you go and read the one with your name on it, Christiana?"

Why don't I? Why would I want to be reminded of all those things? I'm much rather the King forgot about them! But I can't resist having a look, so I go forward slowly and get the piece of paper with my name on it.

Christiana is the oldest, so will she have more things on her list? How many more? Or will it be one of her brothers who has the longest list?

"There's nothing written on it!" I say in surprise.

"Maybe you weren't listening just now," Greatheart says with a smile. "Because his Son died on the Cross, the King offers forgiveness and cleansing to everyone who asks. His Son was punished instead of you, so all those things are washed away, and the paper is blank."

I understand now what it means to be forgiven by the King. I break down in tears and kneel in front of the Cross to say thank you. I don't look at my brothers and Mercy, but I can hear them doing the same, for **every piece of paper is blank**.

The time slips quickly away, and we feel almost sorry when we have to leave this quiet resting place.

The road leads to the foot of a steep hill, and seems to go right up to the top. It's marked *The Way of the King*. Greatheart says this is Hill Difficulty, and he shows us two paths made by the evil prince, both blocked off with posts and chains. One path is marked *Danger*, and it leads into a dark forest, and the other is marked *Destruction* and goes towards some dangerous mountains.

"Christian was here when two boys were lost along those paths," Greatheart tells us, "but he chose to climb the King's path up the hill. Since then, the King has sent men to put these warnings across the wrong paths. Even so, some pilgrims take no notice of them, because the paths look so easy."

As we go up the hill, Greatheart holds onto James, and the rest of us help each other as much as we can. The track is steep and rough, and the sun beats down fiercely on our heads.

Presently Mercy groans loudly. "What a dreadful way up. I don't think I can walk another step. Let's sit down for a few minutes."

"We can't rest here," Greatheart says, "but don't worry. We're near a place the King has made for his pilgrims. Just keep hold of my hand, James. You've climbed bravely, and we're already past the worst. And you too, Joseph. Hold onto my other hand."

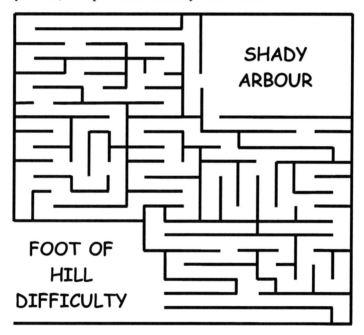

Can you get from the foot of Hill Difficulty to the shady arbour – without getting lost on the way up?

James looks happier when he hears Greatheart's words. Clasping his fingers tightly round those of his guide, James climbs briskly, and in a few minutes a pleasant shelter made of branches and leaves comes in sight, and we hurry towards it.

"You see," Greatheart tells us, "the King's Son has travelled this path himself, so he knows how hard it is, and understands why pilgrims need a resting place." He calls Joseph and James and asks them how they like their pilgrimage.

"I didn't like it at all just now," Joseph says, sounding very grown up, "but I must thank you for helping me."

We sit quietly in the King's shelter, eating the food and drinking the refreshing drink that Interpreter gave us, and talking happily together. Greatheart stands in the doorway.

"We mustn't rest too long," he warns us. "We still have some distance to go, and the sun will soon be setting."

Joseph and James spring up at once, and start off ahead of everyone. I hear them whispering to each other that they won't mind if they *do* meet a lion.

"Greatheart says the King is good, and we know he took care of Christian," I hear Joseph say.

James agrees. "And if we love him, I don't think there's any need to feel frightened."

When I see my two young brothers set off so quickly, I try to keep up with them. We didn't finish the bottle of refreshing drink just now, and I feel thirsty. I suddenly realize I must have left it in the King's shelter where we were eating.

I call to Samuel, and ask him to run back to look for it. While we're waiting, Greatheart says, "It seems to be a forgetting place for some pilgrims."

He tells us about pilgrims who had to turn back to look for something they left there. I ask Greatheart why that should be.

"It's because they're careless," Greatheart tells me. "They get tired climbing the hill, and their rest makes them feel comfortable and happy. But some pilgrims sit there too long, and forget about the King – or even fall asleep. Then they jump up in such a hurry that they're almost sure to drop something without noticing."

What do Christiana and the others have that they might have left behind?

Read this in a mirror, or through the other side of the page.

Samuel returns with the bottle in his hand, and before going any further we all make sure we have our **Rolls of Faith**.

The sun sets while we're climbing the hill. Suddenly Greatheart stops. "Lions!" he says say, signalling to us to stay back.

"Where?" we all ask together in fright.

Greatheart laughs. "I didn't mean to alarm you," he says, "but this is where Christian met two boys running back down the hill. They frightened him by saying they'd seen two lions on the hill."

"Are the lions here now?" Joseph asks.

Greatheart stands with his sword in his hands. "Yes, but there's no need to be scared of them."

Joseph looks at his three brothers. "I don't want to meet a lion," he says shakily. "It might be *very* fierce. We'd better keep behind Greatheart."

"You loved going in front when there was no danger, and now you want to go last," Greatheart says to them, but I know he's only joking.

It's nearly dark now. As we go forward slowly, two lions jump out of the bushes and roar loudly. Joseph and James scream and begin to shake with fear. They hide behind Greatheart, who has drawn his sword ready to strike the lions if they spring forward.

"The beasts are chained," Greatheart says after a moment.

I can see the chains now, glistening in the darkness. "The path between them looks very narrow," I say, trying to sound brave so as not to worry my brothers.

"Keep in a single line in the center of the path," Greatheart tells us.

Mercy gasps and puts her hand to her mouth. "Look, there's a terrible giant standing behind the lions."

Greatheart stops. "I know who he is," he tells us. "His name is Grim. He's made a home for himself here, and he's taught the lions to frighten any pilgrims who are passing."

Giant Grim sees us and steps into the narrow path, holding the manes of the two lions. Greatheart strides boldly forward, but we all stand back, waiting to see what is going to happen.

"What business have you to walk on this path?" the giant roars.

Greatheart raises his sword, "I am taking these young pilgrims to the Celestial City."

"This isn't the way to the City," Grim shouts "If you try to get past, and I will make my lions tear you in pieces."

Greatheart keeps on his way, and we creep after him. His armour glints in the shadows. In a moment his sword flashes through the air, and the giant moves back a few paces.

"Do you think you can *kill* me on my own ground?" Giant Grim shouts at us.

"This path belongs to the King," Greatheart tells him. "Stand and defend yourself, Grim. If you won't let these young pilgrims pass, I will fight you for them."

These are the lions at the top of Hill Difficulty.

Beyond them Christiana and her brothers can see the House Beautiful, but they have to pass the lions before they can get there!

What can Christiana and her brothers now see more clearly?

Greatheart raises his sword as Giant Grim stoops down to unfasten **the lions' chains.** But before the giant can do anything, Greatheart's sharp weapon crashes through the giant's helmet and he falls to his knees. He tries to get up, but with another blow from his sword Greatheart cuts off one of the giant's arms. Giant Grim roars so loudly that his voice scares us all, and we're glad to see him on the ground.

With a powerful blow from his sword, Greatheart cuts off the giant's head. James says, "Wow!" and Greatheart turns round to look for us. Mercy has hidden her face, but I was watching every moment of the battle.

Greatheart calls us forward. "We're nearly at the House Beautiful.," he says. "Keep close to me and the lions won't hurt you. Their master is dead, and they're too frightened to spring at anyone."

We follow Greatheart to the lodge of the large house. A man holding a lantern looks out of a window and asks who we are.

"Greetings, Watchful. I have brought some pilgrims here to stay," Greatheart says. "I know I'm late, but the giant who used to look after the lions caused us some trouble."

"Used to look after the lions?" Watchful asks. "Do you mean to say Giant Grim is dead?"

"Greatheart cut his arm off," Joseph said.

"And then he cut the giant's head off," James adds. "It was ever so exciting."

It's excitement I could have done without, but I'm glad the danger is over – not just for us, but for other pilgrims who will be coming this way later.

"Are you going to stay as well, Greatheart?" Watchful asks.

James goes close to Greatheart and grips his hand, "Please, please stay with us. I'll never forget how brave you've been, and how much you've helped us."

"I will go with you gladly," Greatheart tells him, "but I have to go back tonight. I'll tell Interpreter what you say, and perhaps he will let me come to you again. So, good Christiana, Mercy and my brave boys, farewell."

Greatheart is soon out of sight, for it's now completely dark.

Watchful tells us the big house is called the House Beautiful, and a family of four sisters live there. He takes us there and rings the doorbell. The young woman who answers the door goes quickly back inside the house with Watchful's message, leaving us outside. I hear my name being mentioned in great excitement.

How do the sisters in the House Beautiful know about Christiana?

A girl who says her name is Prudence hurries out with two other girls to welcome us. Prudence explains that **they heard about me from Christian**, and are excited to know that I'm here now. She tells us that their oldest sister, Discretion, has gone away to work for the King in another place.

Prudence's two sisters introduce themselves as Piety and Charity. They kiss us in welcome, and this time even the boys seem to welcome their attention. We can stay with them for a month, to rest and learn about the King.

I'm worried about Matthew. My three other brothers enjoy listening to stories of the King and his Son, but Matthew stays out of the room. Every morning when he gets up he says his head aches, and he often feels so sick and weak he finds it hard to stand.

Today he can hardly lift his head from his pillow when I go to wake him. I run back to my room to finish dressing, so I can ask Prudence what to do. Prudence sends at once for a doctor, an old man called Dr. Skill. He arrives quickly, and I take him up to see my brother.

Matthew is lying in bed, and Joseph is sitting by him, for the two are fond of each other.

"What has he been eating?" Dr. Skill asks.

"Nothing but healthy food," I tell him.

The doctor shakes his head. "He has been eating some sort of poison, and if the medicine I give him won't take effect, he will die,"

I feel so worried that I'm unable to speak, but Samuel cries out, "It must be the berries that were hanging over the wall, after we went through the Wicket Gate. Matthew ate some. Remember, Christiana, you made us throw them away?"

I remember now. "I told him not to eat them," I say, "but he wouldn't listen to me, and kept putting them into his mouth."

"Ah," Dr. Skill says, "I knew he had eaten something poisonous. That fruit is worse than any other, for it grows in the evil prince's own garden."

I feel tears running down my cheeks, for Matthew is looking so white. "What can I do for him?" I ask. "How could I have been so stupid as to let him eat those berries?"

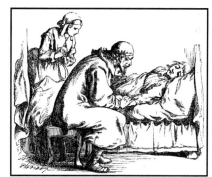

When Dr. Skill sees how frightened I am, he speaks gently. "Do not be too unhappy, Christiana. I have some of the King's medicine with me. If Matthew didn't eat too much fruit, it will do him good."

Dr. Skill prepares some pills and tries to get Matthew to swallow them. But Matthew refuses, even though he's groaning with stomach pain and saying he feels as though he's being pulled to pieces inside.

"Come on," the doctor says, "you have to take them."

Still Matthew refuses.

How would you make Matthew swallow the pills?

"Matthew, do as the doctor tells you," I say firmly.

"I'll be sick," Matthew complains. "Then they'll all come up again."

I pick up one of the pills and touch it on my tongue. It tastes slightly of honey, but has no strong flavor. "Matthew," I say firmly, "if you love me, and if you love your brothers, and if you love Mercy and love your own life, *take your medicine!*"

I know I sound rather strict, but it works. Matthew sits up and swallows the pills. Almost immediately he has to rush to the bathroom. He comes back rather embarrassed, but he's so excited to be feeling well again that he goes off to tell Prudence, Piety and Charity how he's been healed.

"I'd like to keep some of those pills with me," I tell Dr. Skill, and he's willing to prepare some and tell me how and when to use them. It seems they will heal almost any sickness in a true pilgrim.

I decide it was probably a good thing for Matthew that he suffered so much, for he now seems more ready to listen to my advice. He even agrees to let Prudence teach him, and he comes to her with my other brothers, asking her to explain things he doesn't understand about the King and his Son.

* * *

The time passes pleasantly and, toward the end of the month, Joseph reminds me that we want Greatheart to guide us to the Celestial City.

"He was so good to us, and he's so brave," my brother says. "How can we find out if Interpreter will let him come?"

"I will write to him," I say.

So I write a letter and give it to Watchful, who sends it with a messenger to the house of Interpreter. In the evening we hear a knock at the door. Greatheart has arrived. Joseph and James run to cling on to him, and I'm pleased to see he's still wearing his armour.

We leave the House Beautiful, and Greatheart leads us safely through a scary place called the Dark Valley. He says Christian fought the Destroyer here, but today Greatheart calls to the King, who keeps us safe.

We reach the end of the valley and Greatheart points to a cave. "A giant lives in there now," he says. "He knows me and he hates me. Whenever I bring pilgrims out of the valley he tries to stop us."

We draw near the cave, and the giant's massive head looks out. He rushes out waving a large club, and shouts angrily, "How often have you been told not to do these things, Greatheart?"

"To do what things?" Greatheart asks.

What is the giant's name?

The giant is called Maul, a name that means he hurts people by knocking them about – which is why he has a sword in his belt and such a large club in his hand. This is what he looks like. There are three changes in the second picture. One is very easy to spot, but can you find all three?

Giant Maul's club is missing, and so is the handle of the sword on his belt. The third change is to the buttons on the top of his tunic, below his neck.

"You know exactly what I mean," the giant roars angrily, "and I'm putting a stop to it." He seizes his great club and climbs down the rocky path towards us. "You catch men, women and children, and lead them to a strange country far away from my master's kingdom. That is what you do."

"I am a servant of the King," Greatheart calls. "It is my duty to help people find the Way to the King. If you want to fight me because I obey the King, I'm ready for you."

Giant Maul rushes at Greatheart, and strikes him such a terrible blow with his club that Greatheart falls on his knees. I scream in fright, for I think our faithful guide is about to be killed. But Greatheart springs up and hits the giant's arm with his sword.

"I'm going to kill you, Greatheart," Giant Maul roars. "Then I'm going to take these pilgrims back to my prince, and get a big reward."

I know deep down that the King won't leave Greatheart to fight on his own. When the fight begins again, I can see Greatheart's strength and courage increasing every moment.

Maul's power is failing, and he can no longer hold his heavy club. As it falls from his hands, Greatheart thrusts his sword through the giant's chest. In a few moments

Greatheart stands alone on the pathway, the giant dead at his feet.

Greatheart raises his sword and cuts off the giant's head with a single blow. We start to cheer, for although the fight was scary to watch, we know the giant was one of the King's terrible enemies, and it's right for Greatheart to kill him.

A little distance from the cave we reach a small hill. Greatheart tells us it's time to take a rest, and see what lies ahead. As we sit comfortably on the grass, I turn to Greatheart. "Were you frightened when the giant hit you with his club?" I ask.

Greatheart smiles. "At times. But I knew the King would help me, because I was only doing my duty. The King's Son was once wounded, but he conquered in the end, and he won't let his servants be defeated if we're faithful to him."

I can see some huge bruises on Greatheart's arms. I ask him if he's badly hurt.

"Not badly," he says. "**The cuts and bruises haven't Hurt me badly, but Even if they never heal, Keep In mind that it is No good running away from Giants.** I will always remember that I received them fighting for ..."

Who did Greatheart receive them for?

The answer is in the capital letters.

Greatheart received his wounds fighting for **THE KING.**

Later that day we meet an old man called Mr. Honest, and he wants to walk with us. He tells us he once knew someone called Mr. Fearing, and wonders what happened to him. Greatheart says he knew him too, and tells Mr. Honest what happened after Fearing started through the Wicket Gate.

Greatheart says that Goodwill wrote a letter for Fearing to take to Interpreter, asking Interpreter to send a guide to go with him all the way to the Celestial City. But Fearing spent several days and nights in the cold outside Interpreter's gates before anyone knew he was there. Then one morning Greatheart happened to see him from one of the windows, and went down to speak to him. Fearing was weak for want of food, but he brought out Goodwill's letter, and after a little trouble Greatheart persuaded him to enter the house.

"And did you stay with Fearing all the way after that?" Mr. Honest asks.

Greatheart nods. "All the way to the Celestial City. Fearing was pleased when we came to the Cross, and stayed there a long time lost in thought. Whatever he was thinking, it seemed to cheer him up. He didn't mind Hill Difficulty, or the lions each side of the path. He wasn't afraid of such things. He was only afraid the King would think he wasn't fit to be a pilgrim."

"Did you and Fearing stay at the House Beautiful?" I ask. I have many happy memories of that place.

"Fearing loved it there," Greatheart says. "He was too

shy to have much to do with the four sisters, or with their other guests, but he liked to sit in the corner and listen to them talking."

Mr. Honest smiles. "How did he get on in the Dark Valley?" he asks.

"I was afraid it would be terrible for him," Greatheart says. "And indeed it was, but the King didn't allow him to be troubled in the way many pilgrims are. I never saw the valley so light or so quiet at any other time. In Vanity Fair he was angry at the things he saw around him, but he was braver there than anywhere, and was ready to fight the enemies of the King at every turn. However, we passed through the town without being hurt, and after travelling slowly for some time we crossed the Enchanted Ground, and came to the Land of Beulah."

"Fearing must have been happy when he saw the Gates of the Celestial City," Mr. Honest says.

Greatheart shakes his head. "Not at first. He wandered along the bank of the Dark River, looking across at the bright walls, and saying that he was sure he'd never be received there. He kept saying he'd be lost in the deep water. But when the message came for him to go across, I went down to watch. The water was so low that he went over easily. Then the angels met him on the other side, and I saw him no more."

Mr. Honest is glad to hear of his old friend's pilgrimage, and to know he reached the Celestial City safely.

This is Mr. Honest. There are three changes in the next picture. Can you spot them?

Be careful, because what looks like two things is only one!

His sword has gone (both ends, so this only

counts as one), the top of his staff is shorter, and the branch in top left corner is missing.

I say, "I thought I was the only person who's afraid that perhaps the King won't receive them. I feel afraid so often."

"So do I," Mercy whispers.

"And I do," Matthew admits. "And then I think maybe the King will be angry with me for even thinking it."

"No," Greatheart assures us, "the King won't be angry. I think all good pilgrims feel anxious sometimes."

Mr. Honest turns and looks at each one of us. "If anyone imagines they're good enough to be admitted to the Celestial City, it shows they aren't the King's true servants," he says.

My two youngest brothers are complaining that they're feeling tired after their long day, and I have to admit I'm exhausted. The sun has already set, and I keep thinking of the two giants Greatheart has killed – Giant Grim and Giant Maul. We've had enough excitement for one day, and it's time to find somewhere to sleep for the night – preferably indoors.

I ask Greatheart if he knows of a place where we can rest in safety.

"A friend of mine keeps an inn near here," Mr. Honest says. "His name is Gaius. I'm sure he'll let us stay the night."

Gaius welcomes us, and offers us food and beds for the night. He has a young daughter whose name is

Phoebe. Phoebe tells us she has already passed through the Wicket Gate, and now wants to go to the Celestial City. Her father says it would be good for her to travel with us. Phoebe looks almost too small to travel, although she must be about the same age as James – and he's getting on all right. Phoebe insists on going with us, so Gaius asks us to stay for a few days while his daughter prepares for her journey.

When we leave Gaius, Phoebe is with us, and Greatheart says our next stop will be ...

You've read the name before, muddled up like this on a signpost, when Christian reached the same town.

We spend the day crossing the plain, a wild area where nothing much grows. After walking for several hours we see the walls and gates of **Vanity Fair** in the distance. I begin to feel afraid as we get nearer the town of the evil prince.

"Is this where poor Faithful died?" Mercy asks me.

Phoebe is talking to James, but she hears us. "Yes," she pipes up. "It's where the people killed Faithful, and kept Christian shut in a cage."

Mercy gasps, and puts her hand to her mouth. "Do you think they'll put *us* in a cage?"

I feel my face going white, for although Phoebe is small she sounds as though she knows what she's talking about. I try to sound calm. "If we get separated from each other, let's remember how good the King's Son has been to us. We know he's always watching over us. If we have to suffer, we must be brave because we love him."

"Do we *have* to pass through the town?" Mercy asks. "Isn't there a way round?"

Greatheart looks kindly at her. "We *could* go round," he says, "but then we might not find our way onto the right path again."

"I think we should go straight into Vanity Fair," Phoebe says firmly, and although she's the smallest in the group, she seems to have taken charge.

"We'll have to spend the night in the town," Greatheart tells us. "If we pass straight through the town this evening, we won't be able to reach another resting place before dark."

"Where can we sleep?" I ask, trying not to sound too

frightened. "Will the people harm us?"

"I don't think so," Greatheart says. "I've brought many pilgrims safely through Vanity Fair, and I know a good man who keeps an inn. He will let us stay with him, and be pleased to see us, I'm sure. What do you think?"

One by one we all agree to take Greatheart's advice.

"Why would good people want to live in Vanity Fair?" Samuel asks. "Isn't it wrong for them to live there?"

Greatheart shakes his head. "The King has given them work to do there. They help and protect the pilgrims who are passing through, and do their best to make sure no one decides to stay in the town."

Here are Christiana and her brothers at the inn, with Mercy and others. The man who keeps the inn has a most unusual name. Look in your Bible and find the real person with this name, in Acts 21:16. What is he called?

*The name of Greatheart's friend is **Mnason**. The real Mnason was a friend of Saint Paul, and he came from Cyprus. Most people pronounce the name 'Nayson' but some say 'Muh-nayson'. You can say whichever you like!*

Vanity Fair is less busy than I expected, probably because it's now early evening. Some of the people laugh as we pass them, but nobody tries to stop us. We reach the marketplace, and Greatheart shows us the spot where Faithful was killed.

Outside a small inn, Greatheart calls Mnason's name and a man comes out and makes us welcome.

Mnason shows us to a large room set with tables. As soon as we're sitting down, Mr. Honest asks Mnason if there are many good people in Vanity Fair.

"We have a few," Mnason says. He signals to his young daughter called Grace. "Go and tell my friends that I have some pilgrims at my house who would like to meet them here this evening."

Grace runs off and soon comes back with a group of people. Grace has a younger sister called Martha, who is the same age as Joseph. The two sisters seem to be great friends with all these visitors.

Mnason tells us that since the death of Faithful, the people in the town have been much kinder to pilgrims. "I think they still feel guilty for that they did," he says.

The talk turns to our adventures and misadventures so far. Greatheart tells how he killed Giant Grim and Giant Maul.

"Then these pilgrims must stay a while longer," Mnason says, looking at his friends. "We have a dragon outside the town, called False-Teaching. We've just had news that it caught a pilgrim this evening."

"And you'd like us help rescue the pilgrim and kill the dragon?" Samuel asks. "Let's all go now."

I look at my brothers. Matthew says that he'll help, while Joseph and James look excited. Mercy and Phoebe probably feel as I do, for we all smile vaguely.

"We must wait until the morning when it's light," Greatheart says. "It will be too dangerous to go if we cannot see the way ahead."

Mnason agrees. "I'll arrange for us to have an early breakfast. It's no good trying to fight a dragon on an empty stomach. By the way," he adds, "you might as well know. The dragon has seven heads – on seven *very* long necks!"

* * *

It's the early morning now, and we're standing outside Mnason's inn in the dawn light. Joseph and James are at the front, to hear what Mnason has to say. Mnason tells us that the dragon lives in a large forest close to Vanity Fair.

I'm feeling a little afraid. If the people of Vanity Fair are terrified of the dragon, what can *we* do?

"There will be no danger if you all keep close to me," Greatheart explains. "The King told me in a dream last night that we have nothing to fear – as long as we go in his name. He has even provided weapons for us."

"For James as well?" I cry in alarm, as my youngest brother rubs his hands in excitement. "Isn't he too young to fight?"

"The King's swords can be used by everyone," Greatheart says. "Even the youngest pilgrim. You are all to come with us."

* * *

We're inside the forest now, in a place where a rocky hill rises high above the trees. Suddenly Mnason raises a hand to tell us to stay where we are. Everybody stops talking. I can feel my heart beating faster.

Mnason points to the entrance to a large cave a little way up the hill. "This is the lair of False-Teaching," he whispers.

It's strange, but now I can see the cave I don't feel quite so frightened. We climb silently, higher and higher among the rocks, until we are near the entrance.

We can hear someone shouting for help, and the voice seems to be coming from inside the cave. Without warning, a head on the end of a long neck darts out. Six more heads follow, then the scaly green body of the dragon, so we can see all seven heads and long necks of this terrible creature.

The dragon stands in the mouth of the cave, its heads waving around in rage. It utters seven roars that shake the hillside as it clambers over the large rocks to attack us.

False-Teaching looks so powerful that I know it could kill us all if we weren't armed with the King's weapons. As the fight begins, Greatheart climbs above the cave, unseen by the dragon.

As the beast roars its terrifying roar, Greatheart leaps down onto its back and slashes his sword across one of the long necks. Still joined to its neck, the head rolls past us, dripping blood. We all jump out of the way.

Screaming with pain, the dragon rushes back into the cave. I look down at the head, afraid it will bite us, but it's completely still.

How many heads are left on the dragon? One? Two? Three? Four? More than four?

"There are still six heads left," James whispers, his small sword raised in his hand, ready for another battle if the dragon gets this far.

The next attack comes while Greatheart is climbing down from the rocks. The dragon is expecting Greatheart to be above, and it looks up with all six remaining heads on the end of their long necks.

Greatheart is to one side and slashes off one head, and then another. False-Teaching is wild with a mixture of rage and pain, its long necks waving around.

Mnason hurries forward to kill it, but Matthew and Samuel get there first. The terrible roars suddenly stop as the last head rolls down the hill, and dragon's body collapses in the cave entrance.

Joseph and James are the first to enter the cave, and they come out with the trapped pilgrim. We are glad to see he's unhurt, and take him back to the town to stay with Mnason until he's well again.

When Mnason's friends in Vanity Fair hear about the death of False-Teaching, they tell us they're glad about it, and even the evil prince's citizens can't help thanking us for our bravery. We get to know many people in the town over the next few days, and try to help some who are most in need.

We work together to feed and clothe the poor, and Mercy is especially hard-working. Mnason says she's a fine example of how pilgrims should behave. Phoebe, and Mnason's two daughters Grace and Martha, set us all a good example by showing kindness to everyone, and I keep hearing people speak well of us.

At last the time comes for us to continue our journey. Mnason says Grace and Martha entered the Wicket Gate some time ago, and have been waiting for a guide to help them on the rest of their way to the Celestial City. He asks Greatheart if he will allow them to travel with us.

Greatheart says he'll be pleased to help, which is good news for me – because now the boys will no longer outnumber the girls.

Many of the King's servants come to the gates of Vanity Fair to bid us farewell, and give us gifts for our journey. The King has been so good in letting me meet people who are so kind to us.

"I was afraid they'd shut us in their cage," I say to Mercy as we leave.

"So was I," she says. "But we made new friends there, and the King kept us safe."

Greatheart is telling us about a place which is only a day's journey from Vanity Fair. He says we'll be able to spend tonight in its quiet meadows, and that sounds good.

The place is called:

We are glad to rest by **the River of the Water of Life**, but Greatheart warns us that we must not stay there more than a day, or it will be hard to get going again. We bathe in its water, and all of us set off early the next morning.

In the middle of the day we reach a stile leading to a place called By-Path Meadow. We tell Greatheart our feet are hurting, for the road has been rough with sharp stones, and ask if we can walk on the smooth path just the other side of the hedge.

"We can get through the hedge later," I say. "I'm sure it will be easy to get back onto this path."

Greatheart shows us a stone with some words cut into the smooth surface:

Over this stile is the way to Doubting Castle,
which is kept by Giant Despair.
He despises the King of the Celestial Country,
and seeks to destroy his holy pilgrims.
The Key of Promise opens all the giant's locks.

Greatheart explains why Christian and his friend Hopeful put the stone here by the side of the road. He tells us how Christian and Hopeful went to sleep in By-Path Meadow in a storm, and were caught the next morning by Giant Despair. He tells us about Despair's wife, Diffidence, and how she wanted Christian and Hopeful killed. I feel so ashamed that I wanted to take everyone on the wrong path.

"Why doesn't someone kill the giants?" Samuel asks,

and I agree it sounds an excellent idea. I'm getting quite used to seeing giants and other monsters having their heads cut off, even if there is a lot of blood and noise.

"We're not strong enough, are we?" James says, looking at Greatheart. "But *you* could kill the *biggest* giant."

Greatheart smiles. "Only with the help of the King," he says. "And the King will help *you* if you trust in him."

"So *we* could kill Giant Despair – and his wife?" James asks in a hushed voice.

"Yes."

"Come on, let's try!" Joseph shouts eagerly. "Those giants have killed lots of pilgrims."

Matthew's eyes look surprisingly bright. "Perhaps there are some pilgrims shut up in the castle," he says. "If there are, we can rescue them."

Matthew seems to have gained a lot of courage lately. Perhaps we've all got bolder. "But isn't it wrong to leave the Way of the King?" I ask.

Giant Despair caught Christian and Hopeful in By-Path Meadow, and locked them in Doubting Castle. Will it be any safer for the pilgrims to cross the stile now?

"If the boys really wish to fight with Giant Despair and his wife, the King won't be displeased," Greatheart tells me. "Christian and Hopeful went over the stile because, like you, Christiana, they thought the way would be easier. That's why they fell into trouble."

The boys shout that they'll follow Greatheart to Doubting Castle, and Mr. Honest says he must certainly go with them. Greatheart gives me and Mercy a sword each, and tells us to stay back with the Phoebe, Grace and Martha, to protect them if the enemy comes.

I hold my sword tightly, happy to be given this important job. I hope I won't let anyone down. Mercy smiles at me, holding her sword in the air. Well, we can certainly try our best – and of course call to the King for help.

Greatheart and his group go out of sight. It's quite late in the day when they return, dragging the heads of two giants along the path. They also have two pilgrims walking with them. One is a man with a sad and weary face, and the other a young woman. Samuel explains they've been lying in the dark dungeon for six days. The man looks pale and faint, and lies on the grass while Phoebe helps me rub his cold hands. While we're doing this, Grace and Martha make sure he eats some food.

At last the man sits up and thanks us. He says his name is Despondency, and he was travelling to the Celestial City with his young daughter Much-Afraid. His daughter was doing her best to help him, but they quickly lost all hope of being rescued from Doubting Castle.

I notice Matthew's sword still has blood on the end.

Maybe he's left it on there so I can see it. "You did well to kill the giants," I say to him. "I'm proud of you." This evening Matthew looks older and stronger than ever. Come to that, we're all a lot older than when we first set out.

Matthew's eyes sparkle. "When we got to the castle we knocked as loudly we could. Giant Despair comes to the door, and he has his wife Diffidence with him." He glances at the two heads on the ground. "That's her," he says, pointing. "The one with the long hair."

"I guessed," I say.

"Well," Matthew continues, "Giant Despair demands to know who we are. So Greatheart shouts, 'It is I, Greatheart, one of the King's guides for pilgrims. I have come to cut off your heads and destroy Doubting Castle.'"

"That's exactly what he said," James says, jumping up and down. "But Giant Despair didn't seem worried. He said no one could kill him."

"He was wearing armour," Samuel explains. "He had a steel helmet and breastplate."

"And metal shoes on his feet," Joseph says.

"And a huge great club," James adds. "His wife Diffidence joined in the fight, but one of us killed her with one great poke from his sword!"

"Mr. Honest did it," James says. "He's the bravest man I've ever seen – apart from Greatheart, of course."

I look at the old man, who just shrugs and smiles modestly.

"That wasn't the end of it, though," James says, waving his small sword. "We couldn't kill Giant Despair. I stuck my sword into his leg, but he didn't seem to notice." And he thrust it forward fiercely, just in case none of us understood.

"I slashed his arms and he started pouring blood, but it was Greatheart who finished him off," Matthew says, managing to get a word in at last. "We thought Giant Despair had as many lives as a cat, but we knew he was dead when Greatheart cut his head off."

I nod. "That does tend to show a giant is dead," I say dryly. "Anyway, it's all over now." And I can't say I'm sorry to have missed the fight.

Mercy stands close to Matthew and smiles at him. "You must have been fearless," she says. "I'm glad *we* didn't fall into the giant's hands." She turns to the two pilgrims who have just been rescued. Her face grows serious. "Much-Afraid looks as if she might die even now," she whispers.

I remember the pills Dr. Skill gave me, and Much-Afraid swallows them with difficulty. Soon she smiles and gets to her feet.

"You will quickly grow stronger if we take care of you," Greatheart tells her confidently.

"Did you destroy the castle?" I ask.

James is nearly bursting with excitement. "We busted

down all the gates and doors. You should have seen us."

Matthew's eyes shine as he puts his sword back into its sheath. "That was a good fight," he says, "but Greatheart says there will be more battles on the path ahead."

Greatheart is putting the giants' heads on two wooden posts. James asks him why he's doing it.

"To warn other pilgrims not to go near Doubting Castle," he explains.

"But the giants are dead and their doors and gates are smashed down," James says, with a puzzled frown. "So surely the danger has gone."

Greatheart says it will be dangerous here again, because:

Oth erg ian tsw ill soo nre bui ldt hem

You read from left to right, but the spaces are in the wrong places.

"True." Greatheart pushes Despair's head down firmly onto the post. "But you can be sure that **other giants will soon rebuild them**, and cause just as much trouble as these two."

We are going on again, with Greatheart leading the way. He suddenly signals for us to stop. A man is standing with his sword in his hand, his face covered in blood.

Greatheart asks him what happened. The man is tall and strong, and I feel sure I've seen him before.

"My name is Valiant-for-Truth," the man says. "Three men came attacked me, because I'm a pilgrim like yourselves. They drew their swords, and I drew mine, and we've been fighting for nearly three hours. I suppose they must have heard you coming, for they suddenly turned and ran away."

"That was a hard battle, three men to one," Greatheart tells him.

"Hard, yes," Valiant-for-Truth says, "but I knew I was fighting against my King's enemies, and that gave me courage."

Greatheart looks surprised. "Why didn't you cry for help? Some of the King's servants might have been near enough to hear you."

"I cried to the King himself," Valiant-for-Truth says, "and I'm sure he answered me by sending you."

This is Valiant-for-Truth. There are three changes in the bottom picture. Can you spot them?

The tip of Valiant-for-Truth's sword is missing, the sword on ground has moved, and the end of the cloak by Valiant-for-Truth's knees has gone.

Greatheart looks at Valiant-for-Truth in surprise. "You fought for three hours? Weren't you ready to drop with exhaustion?"

"As I fought, my sword seemed to become part of my arm."

"You've been courageous," Greatheart says. "You must finish your journey with us. We'll all be glad of your company."

We make the soldier welcome. I wash his wounds, and Mercy and Phoebe help me bind them up. Grace and Martha get the boys to help them prepare some food, and we tell Valiant-for-Truth he must rest, for he's been in a bad fight.

* * *

It's the evening now, and we've to start once more on our journey.

I make sure I'm walking just behind Greatheart and Valiant-for-Truth, so I can hear everything the soldier says in answer to Greatheart's questions. He's telling Greatheart he once lived in the City of Destruction, and I keep wondering where I've seen him before.

"What made you become a pilgrim?" Greatheart asks.

"I have a son," Valiant-for-Truth says. "When his mother, my wife, went to live with the King, he kept talking about the Celestial City. One morning he started on a journey to find the King, and I was too busy to stop him and bring him back."

"What is your son's name?" Greatheart asks.

I listen for the answer, for now I feel sure I know who this soldier is.

Who is Valiant-for-Truth?

C h - i - t - a - s - a - h - r

"My son's name is Christian," the soldier says. "Someone called Truth told me how Christian fought with giants. Truth also said Christian was made welcome at all the King's lodgings, and when he came to the Gates of the Celestial City he was received with the sound of trumpets and a company of angels. As Truth told the story, my heart told me to go after my son, for my work could not delay me any longer from finding the King. So here I am, on my way." He pauses and smiles, in spite of the cuts on his arms and face from the fight.

Greatheart nods. "You came through the Wicket Gate then?"

"Indeed, yes," Valiant-for-Truth tells us all. "Truth told me that it would all be for nothing if I did not enter at the Gate."

"Do you remember me?" I ask shyly. I used to be rather afraid of Christian's father, for he always seemed too important to speak to someone like me.

"Why, yes," he says with a friendly wink. "You are Christian's friend, Christiana." He looks at the four boys. "And these, I think, must be your brothers. Well, I have to say how much you've all grown since I last saw you. It gladdens my heart to think that Christian will be greeting you, as well as me."

"And you've not been sorry you started out?" I ask.

Valiant-for-Truth smiles at me. "No, indeed not, Christiana."

Greatheart claps his hands. "Come on, everybody, and pay attention. We are now getting near the Enchanted Ground. We all have to keep each other awake."

The Enchanted Ground is a strange place. As we enter it, we feel different. I begin to yawn and Greatheart is quick to notice.

"Be careful, Christiana," he calls. "If you sit down to rest and fall asleep, you may never wake up again."

This frightens me so much that I feel wide awake – but only for a minute or two. I'm already starting to feel sleepy again.

Imagine you're in charge of the pilgrims.

Who would you put at the tnorf

and who would you ask to go at the kcab

as you all cross the Enchanted Ground?

Greatheart goes to the **front**, for he's the guide. Valiant-for-Truth follows at the **back** as the guard, in case some dragon or giant or thief attacks us from behind. Everyone who has a sword holds it in their hands, for we know this is a dangerous place.

We cheer each other up as well as we can, but a great mist and darkness is now hiding everything from sight. We can't even see each other, and keep calling out to be sure of staying together.

Greatheart and Valiant-For-Truth sound as though they're getting on well enough, but the rest of us are finding it painful. We keep huffing and puffing as we trip over a bush here, and get our shoes stuck in the soft ground there. James shouts that he's lost one of his shoes in the mud, but Matthew manages to get it back for him, even though he has to do it all by touch.

It's a great relief when the mist clears a little, and we see an arbour where we all want to rest. It's well built and covered with green branches, with seats inside. There's even a bed covered with soft, springy moss.

"Make sure you all keep out of that shelter," Greatheart calls. "It's been built by the evil prince to trap pilgrims who stop when they feel too tired to go on."

I certainly feel like stopping for a bit, but of course I don't – not after that warning. It's completely dark as we press on, and Greatheart tells us to wait while he lights his lamp. "I need to be absolutely sure of what lies ahead of us," he says.

Greatheart holds his lantern up to read a map he's taken from his pocket. We all gasp when we see a pit right in the middle of our path.

"The King's enemies have dug this," Greatheart says. "It's full of water and mud. It may be extremely deep, and if you fall in, you could be lost forever."

Carefully, by the light from the lamp, we make our way around the muddy pit one at a time, trying not to look down into it.

"Keep close," Greatheart warns. "We're nearly out of the Enchanted Ground, and we'll soon be safe in ..."

Where will they be safe?

It's where Christian waited, before going to the Celestial City.

We're safely through the Enchanted Ground at last, and are **in the Land of Beulah.** The sun is shining, and Greatheart tells us it shines all day, but it never burns. I'm feeling tired after our journey, so I decide to lie down and rest in a house we've been given on the edge of an orchard.

Almost as soon as I get to sleep, the sound of bells on the other side of a wide river wakes me up. People are blowing trumpets, but I don't feel like complaining, for the music is so lovely.

I go to the window and see three angels walking along the road with a group of pilgrims. As they pass us, from the open window I can hear the angels saying words of comfort to the pilgrims.

My ears are now filled with beautiful sounds, and I know I've never felt this peaceful before. I can almost imagine I'm in the Celestial City, even though it's on the other side of what people are calling the Dark River.

I go out into the orchard, and some children run up to me with bunches of flowers. They have enough for Mercy, and yet more for Phoebe, Grace and Martha. My four brothers are sitting together, talking under an apple tree – and I don't expect they want flowers.

I think perhaps Matthew will make a good teacher, as he's become so wise lately. He smiles when I go across and tell him this.

"I'd like to be a teacher, if the King chooses the work for me," he says.

I tell Samuel he'll make a good soldier like Greatheart.

"To guide and protect the pilgrims?" he asks. "Yes," he says thoughtfully, "that would be the best work of all. But I can never be as good as Greatheart."

James says, "I think Greatheart was always a good soldier."

But Joseph says, "I think Greatheart needed to learn from the King."

I sit down with the boys. **"Joseph is right.** Do you think Greatheart was that good at first? He must have been taught how to work for the King. I expect he made all sorts of mistakes at first, but he kept trying to serve the King. You're brave and careful, Samuel. You'll quickly learn to be a good soldier and guide."

Joseph and James tell me they've had enough travelling for a bit, but I can see the journey has done them good. I wonder what the King has in mind for them.

Mercy comes across. "We were so few when we started," she says as she sits with us on the grass. "Now look how many of us there are here in Beulah. Some young and some old, some weak and some strong, and yet the King has cared for us all."

I see Matthew looking at Mercy with a smile on his face, and I wonder what the future has in store for them.

* * *

It is now many years later. I'm looking out of the window, thinking about the past. Matthew has married my best friend Mercy, and together they are teaching young pilgrims, along with three children of their own. More of a surprise was the marriage of Samuel to Grace, the daughter of Mnason. They have a baby boy.

Joseph is engaged to Grace's sister Martha, and they will marry soon. Phoebe, the daughter of Gaius, always seems to be with James. Meeting young Phoebe at the inn of Gaius seems like a distant memory now.

I'm pleased to know that my brothers are with true followers of the King.

Mr. Honest, and some of the other pilgrims we journeyed with, have already crossed the Dark River, and are now at peace in the Celestial City.

Christian's father, Valiant-for-Truth, crossed over a few months ago. He said he was proud to have received so many cuts and injuries for the King. So finally Valiant-for-Truth is with his wife and with his son Christian. Before leaving, he gave his sword to Samuel who is training to be one of the King's soldiers, just like Great-heart.

I keep thinking back to the time when I sat on the hill above the City of Destruction. How different life was for me then. I knew nothing of the love of the King and his Son, and I knew nothing of the joy that is waiting for me now in the Celestial City.

I hear a knock at the door. I open it and an angel stands there with a message from the King.

"Greetings, Christiana," the angel says. "I bring you news that the King is calling you, and wants you to stand in his presence, in clothes of everlasting life."

"I am coming, Lord," I say, "to be with you and bless you for ever."

EPILOGUE

Yes, this really is the end! Well done, if you solved lots of puzzles and answered lots of questions. You can read plenty more about Christian and Christiana in *Pilgrim's Progress – Special Edition*, my longer book for older readers of all ages – even adults. There aren't any puzzles in it, but there are all sorts of extra people they meet, and exciting adventures that haven't been told here. There just hasn't been room for everything.

The story in this book isn't different, it's just shorter. So you will be able to read *Pilgrim's Progress – Special Edition* without finding all sorts of changes to what happens. Maybe one day you will even decide to read John Bunyan's original book.

* * *

Chris Wright is the author and co-author of over thirty books, starting with young fiction for an English Christian publisher in 1966. He has written both fiction and non-fiction, mostly with a Christian theme, for a variety of publishers. Chris is married with three grownup children, and lives in the West Country of England where he is a homegroup leader with his local church.

His website is www.rocky-island.com

MARY JONES AND HER BIBLE

AN ADVENTURE BOOK

(ENDORSED BY BIBLE SOCIETY)

Chris Wright

ISBN: 978-0-9525956-2-5

White Tree Publishing

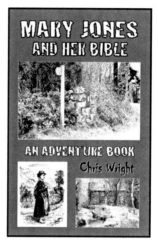

Take part in Mary Jones' adventure! Mary Jones saved for six years to buy a Bible of her own – and after walking 26 miles (over 40km) to get it, she discovered there were none for sale! Mary made her walk alone, barefoot over a mountain pass and through deep valleys in Wales in 1800, at the age of 15.

You can travel with her today in this book as you follow the clues and solve the puzzles. You, too, will get to Bala where Mary travelled, and if you're really quick you may be able to "buy" a Bible just like Mary's!

The true story of Mary Jones and her Bible has captured the imagination for more than 200 years. For this book, Chris Wright has delved deep into the records and come up with the latest facts that are known about Mary.

Packed with puzzles, photographs of real places, and all sorts of fascinating information. If a puzzle is too difficult, or you just don't like puzzles at all, you can turn the page and keep reading. Solving puzzles is part of the fun, but the story is still there to read and enjoy whether you have a go at the puzzles or not. Can you discover the story of Mary Jones?

Endorsed by Bible Society

5.5 x 8.5 inches 158 pages £6.95
Available from bookshops
and major internet stores

AGATHOS,
THE ROCKY ISLAND,
AND OTHER STORIES
Chris Wright
ISBN 978-0-9525956-8-7
White Tree Publishing

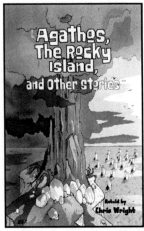

Once upon a time there were two favorite books for Sunday reading: *Parables From Nature* and *Agathos and The Rocky Island.*

These books contained all sorts of short stories, usually with a hidden meaning. In this illustrated book is a selection of the very best of these stories, carefully retold to preserve the feel of the originals, coupled with ease of reading and understanding for today's readers.

Discover the king who sent his servants to trade in a foreign city. The butterfly who thought her eggs would hatch into baby butterflies, and the two boys who decided to explore the forbidden land beyond the castle boundary. The spider that kept being blown in the wind, the soldier who had to fight a dragon, the four children who had to find their way through a dark and dangerous forest. These are just six of the nine stories in this collection. Oh, and there's also one about a rocky island!

This is a book for a young person to read alone, a family or parent to read aloud, Sunday school teachers to read to the class, and even for grownups who want to dip into the fascinating stories of the past all by themselves. Can you discover the hidden meanings? You don't have to wait until Sunday before starting!

5.5 x 8.5 inches 148 pages £5.95
Available from major internet stores

PILGRIM'S PROGRESS
SPECIAL EDITION
Chris Wright
ISBN: 978-0-9525956-7-0
White Tree Publishing

The Special Edition is a much longer version of this book, with extra things happening. It is for all ages and is a great choice for young readers, as well as for families, Sunday school teachers, and anyone who wants to read John Bunyan's *Pilgrim's Progress* in a clear form.

All the old favourites from this book are here: Christian, Christiana, the Wicket Gate, Interpreter, Hill Difficulty with the lions, the four sisters at the House Beautiful, Vanity Fair, Giant Despair, Faithful and Talkative – and, of course, Greatheart. There are also some good and bad characters you haven't met yet.

The first part of the story is told by Christian himself, as he leaves the City of Destruction to reach the Celestial City, and becomes trapped in the Slough of Despond near the Wicket Gate. On his journey he will encounter lions, giants, and a creature called the Destroyer.

Christiana follows along later, and tells her own story in the second part. Not only does Christiana have to cope with her four young brothers, she worries about whether her clothes are good enough for meeting the King. Will she find the dangers in Vanity Fair that Christian found? Will she be caught by Giant Despair and imprisoned in Doubting Castle? What about the dragon with seven heads?

It's a dangerous journey, but Christian and Christiana both know that the King's Son is with them, helping them through the most difficult parts until they reach the Land of Beulah, and see the Celestial City on the other side of the Dark River. This is a story you will remember for ever, and it's about a journey you can make for yourself.

5.5 x 8.5 inches 278 pages £8.95
Available from major internet stores

ZEPHAN AND THE VISION

Chris Wright

ISBN: 978-0-9525956-9-4
White Tree Publishing

An exciting story about the adventures of two angels who seem to know almost nothing – until they have a vision!

Two ordinary angels are caring for the distant Planet Eltor, and they are about to get a big shock – they are due to take a trip to the Planet Earth! This is Zephan's story of the vision he is given before being allowed to travel with Talora, his companion angel, to help two young people fight against the enemy.

Arriving on Earth, they discover that everyone lives in a small castle. Some castles are strong and built in good positions, while others appear weak and open to attack. But it seems that the best-looking castles are not always the most secure.

Meet Castle Nadia and Castle Max, the two castles that Zephan and Talora have to defend. And meet the nasty creatures who have built shelters for themselves around the back of these castles. And worst of all, meet the shadow angels who live in a cave on Shadow Hill. This is a story about the forces of good and the forces of evil. Who will win the battle for Castle Nadia?

The events in this story are based very loosely on John Bunyan's allegory *The Holy War*.

5.5 x 8.5 inches 216 pages £7.95
Available from major internet stores

CPSIA information can be obtained at www.ICGtesting.com
Printed in the USA
BVOW042041231111

276805BV00008B/46/P